THE
WALLCREEPER

Also by Nell Zink

Mislaid

THE WALLCREEPER

Nell Zink

FOURTH ESTATE • *London*

Fourth Estate
An imprint of HarperCollins Publishers
1 London Bridge Street
London SE1 9GF
www.4thestate.co.uk

First published in Great Britain by Fourth Estate in 2015
First published in the United States by Dorothy, a Publishing Project in 2014

1 3 5 7 9 10 8 6 4 2

A catalogue record for this book
is available from the British Library

ISBN 978-0-00-813084-8

Printed and bound in Great Britain by
Clays Ltd, St Ives plc

MIX
Paper from
responsible sources
FSC
www.fsc.org
FSC® C007454

I kill where I please because it is all mine.

—Ted Hughes

I *was looking at the map when Stephen swerved, hit the rock,* and occasioned the miscarriage. Immediately obvious was my sticky forehead. Maybe I was unconscious for a couple of seconds, I don't know. Eventually I saw Stephen poking around the front of the car and said, "Jesus, what was that."

He leaned in at the window and said, "Hey, you're bleeding. Hold on a second." He crossed behind the car, looked both ways, and retrieved the bird from the opposite ditch.

I opened the door and put my feet outside, threw up, and lay down, not in the vomit but near it. The fir tops next to me had their roots at the bottom of a cliff.

"Can I use this bread bag?" Stephen asked. "Tiff? Tiff?" He kneeled next to me. "That was stupid of me. I shouldn't touch you after handling this bird. Can you hear me? Tiff?"

He helped me into the back seat and I lay down on the bread. He said head wounds always bleed like that. I said he should have kept quiet. I lost the ability to see and began to hyperventilate a bit. The car pulled back on to the road. From the passenger seat the wallcreeper said, "Twee."

"Open the bag!" I cried.

"Twee!" it said again.

Stephen pulled over and busied himself with it for a moment. He said, "I thought it was dead. I just wanted to get it off the road. I was going to have it prepared or something, I don't know. You should see its wings. For me it's a lifer. It's like the most wonderful bird. But it's a species of least concern and actually they're all over the place except anyplace you would normally go. I identified it even before I hit it. *Tichodroma muraria!* It was unmistakable, just like they said it would be. So this is great. Dead is not a tick as far as I'm concerned. I identified it before I hit it anyway. It really is unmistakable. You should see it, Tiff. I'm rambling on like this because you might have a concussion and you're not supposed to sleep."

"Put on music."

The wallcreeper protested. "Twee!"

I stayed awake by retching, and Stephen drove defensively but swiftly back to Interlaken.

When I awoke—I mean the next time I was allowed a cup of coffee—Stephen steadied my hand on the mug and said, "I have a surprise for you. But it's in the kitchen."

"I don't think I can get up."

"Well, it can't come in here."

"It will have to wait." I slurped and he winced. I drank more quietly.

"Twee," said the wallcreeper.

"You didn't!" I laughed. But my—what am I going to call it? My down there plays a minor role in several scenes to come. It appeared to be connected to the underside of my stomach with shock cords stretched too tight. I rolled over on my side and coughed. I wasn't pregnant, I noticed. I clenched my hands into claws and cried like a drift log in heavy surf. Stephen put his hands on my ears. Much later he told me he thought if I couldn't hear myself I might stop. He said it reminded him of feedback mounting in an amplifier.

Our first meeting prevented a crime. He saw me standing in front of the open gate of the vault. I had an armful of files, my hips were thrust forward, one wee foot in ballet slippers was rubbing the instep of the other, my skirt was knee-length and plaid and my blouse was white and roomy, and I was thinking: If I move fast, I can grab the files on that stuff they use to euthanize psychotics and be down the stairwell in ten seconds. I was a typist at a pharmaceutical company in Philadelphia. The vault was where the bodies were buried, and there was no one in sight. Except Stephen, who walked up and asked my name.

"Tiffany," he said. "That means a divine revelation. From *theophany*."

"It means a lampshade," I said. "It's a way to get around the problem of putting your light under a bushel. The light and the bushel are one."

He didn't back away. It was one of those moments where you think: We will definitely fuck. It might take a while, though, because Stephen looked as respectable as I did.

He was interviewing for a position in R&D in Berne.

He pretended I was going to be this really difficult and challenging conquest. He wooed me with everything I ever mentioned favorably: Little Debbie marshmallow pies, nasturtiums, the sweet wines so dear to the palate of our shared idol Richard Nixon (a joke), Alban Berg (a joke he didn't get). He had no intention of going to Berne alone.

My parents were unanimous. "He's a keeper," they said. They just about kicked me into bed with him. So the first time we had sex was on their pullout sofa. He was beautiful. It was hypnotic. I was sold.

He warned me that his parents were arty. His father sat me down on the dock behind their house and advised me to enter into a suicide pact effective on Stephen's fiftieth birthday. I said, "If I make it that long," which was the right answer. His mother didn't make it home that weekend. We were married in

Orphans' Court. From the vault to the altar took three weeks. We didn't talk much about what we were doing. We had a deal.

I hadn't wanted to be pregnant. It was just one of those things that happen when newlyweds get drunk. It seemed like something I'd get used to. Losing the baby was more dire than I had dreamed possible. Cause and effect had no relation at all. The effect was way over my head, and beside it, and beyond it. It was a bodily distress. I had no way of putting it into words. So I didn't. Stephen would sit there on the edge of the bed, looking at me, holding my hand, then lie down and tuck himself in. I didn't feel gloomy. I didn't even feel sorry for myself. I didn't tell myself what had happened. If I tell myself stories, I get very sentimental very fast. So I didn't. I moved around slowly, looking at things before I touched them to make sure there was nothing frightening about them. I had no thoughts to speak of. I wanted to be addressed in hushed tones of pity, even by myself. I wanted to hear my own whispers in the next room and know that I was thinking of me.

We didn't have friends yet in Berne really, but his colleague Omar came to look at the wallcreeper. Omar was in Animal Health, so he knew something about birds. Also, he was in pharmaceuticals, so he knew how to keep a secret. He told Stephen the bird would never fly again and that stealing it out of the wild was not of the brainiest.

The next day, I got up and went into the kitchen. The wallcreeper flew across the room, banged into the window, and lay still. Then, as before, it sat up and said, "Twee." It leapt on to its feet like a little karate black belt recovering from a fall. It flicked its wings and tongued a flax seed on the floor.

"I'm worried about it," I said to Stephen on the phone. "It can't get any traction on the wall. It needs pegboard. Then we could feed it. We could, like, put bugs in the holes in the pegboard. I don't like that you're feeding it bacon or whatever this is on the bulletin board. What is this? It's going to pull out the pushpins and get hurt. We have to give it bugs, to prepare it for release into the wild."

"If it gets out, we'll never see it again," Stephen said. "Why don't you go out shopping and buy some curtains? Get white. That would keep it from trying to fly out the window. It's going to get conspicuous if it starts flying around." Which was true. It flew like a giant butterfly, or a tiny bird of paradise, or a nylon propeller fluttering from a kite.

"Scramble it some eggs," Stephen added. "Whatever's in eggs must be in birds. Relax until I get home."

*

After Stephen saw the curtains and screwed the pegboard to the wall, he wanted to have sex standing up in the kitchen. It had been three weeks.

We kissed, but my whatever had not healed. It was hot and dry. (I mean my brain.) I just stood there in a state of mournful passivity while he knelt down and licked me, touching my asshole rhythmically with one finger and petting my thigh in counterpoint. I felt sad. His awkward hands reminded me of the flames around Joan of Arc at the stake. But I knew after we started to have actual sex I would feel better. However, that was before he entered my butt with the rest of his hand followed by his penis and the metaphoric auto-da-fé became a thick one-to-one description of taking a dump.

Now, all my life I had fantasized about being used sexually in every way I could think of on the spur of the respective moment. How naïve I was, I said to myself. In actuality this was like using a bedpan on the kitchen counter. I knew with certainty that "pain" is a euphemism even more namby-pamby than "defilement." Look at Stephen! He thinks he's having sex! Smell his hand! It's touching my hair! I thought, Tiff my friend, we shall modify a curling iron and burn this out of your brain. But I didn't say anything. I acted like in those teen feminist poems where it's date rape if he doesn't read you the Antioch College rules chapter and verse while you're glumly failing to see rainbows. I was still struggling to dissociate myself into an out-of-body experience when Stephen came, crying out like a dinosaur.

I gasped for air, dreading the moment when he would pull out, and thought, Girls are lame.

After a shower with fantasies of pharmaceutical-grade trisodium phosphate and nothing to wash with but gentle pH-negative shower gels, I had recovered sufficiently ... actually I had recovered from everything! I was no longer in love! My sense of depending on Stephen for my happiness had evaporated. Furthermore, I had overcome my fear of intimacy. All intimacy was gone. I didn't care whether Stephen ever understood me. I knew it for a fact. I had just proved it.

In addition, I felt almost nostalgic toward socially acceptable horrors with larger meanings related to reproduction. (As I was to learn, reproductive urges will serve as an alibi for just about anything.) I recalled things I had seen in the hospital that did not admit of euphemism—certain stark natural occurrences that gave the lie to language itself simply because no one, anywhere, absolutely no one in the world, would ever take a notion to claim they were fun. Irredeemable moments with no exchange value whatsoever.

I went to bed and lay propped up on pillows, thinking about it. Stephen came out of the shower and stood naked in the doorway. He was beaming like a god, radiant with abashed joy. "Was I bad?" he asked.

"You were super-bad," I said. He knelt across my chest and eventually sort of fucked my mouth. He was uninhibited, as in inconsiderate. I felt like the Empress Theodora.

Can I get more orifices? I thought. Is that what she meant in the *Historia Arcana*—not that three isn't enough, but that the three on offer aren't enough to sustain a marriage?

Omar and his wife had us over to dinner. She served unaccustomed delicious food and had us sit on unfamiliar comfortable furniture. She wanted to know about the wallcreeper.

"It's beautiful," Stephen said. "I mean, not flashy like ducks or elegant like avocets—"

"Flashy ducks?" Omar objected. He was from Asia.

"There are plenty of flashy ducks here," I said in Stephen's defense. "Relatively speaking."

Stephen said, "Okay, what I mean is, it has this essential duality. It's tiny and gray and you'd never notice it, and then these wings. Woo. You have to see them." He spread his hands like outfielders' mitts and shook them to express his incapacity to understand the wallcreeper. The gesture was like a prayer of desperation, but he never raised his eyes, as if to say, there is no one to appeal to for help, not even me.

It was an effective gesture. Omar's wife leaned back, nodding, believing in the wallcreeper.

Stephen came home one day mad at Omar, who had told him which zoo collects wallcreepers. Omar opined that we would be given amnesty if we surrendered Rudolf voluntarily. He reemphasized that in Asia even the squirrels are flashy and piebald, and no one should get attached to a wild animal for its looks. Omar's job involved feeding caged beagles different chow formulas to see which ones lived longest. The lab record was fourteen years.

Otherwise Stephen was never mad at coworkers. He got along beautifully with his bosses and subordinates. Everyone liked him. They liked his work on the new stent. They admired his pretty wife with the orthodox-Jewish-looking outfits, but hey, not her fault Americans are dowdy. They frowned at her pregnancy no sooner announced than cancelled. One thing he never told them about: birds. The company employed expert tax-evasion consultants, semi-closeted gray-market OTC pirates, hail-fellow-well-met good old boy executives who laughed off multi-million-dollar fines for taking risks that killed people, PR hacks who wrote threatening letters to Nelson Mandela about socialized medicine. They practiced twenty-seven kinds of window-dressing and I had typed letters about them all. But even the veterinarian in regulatory affairs whose life was spent tweaking a children's book about cats that sing opera was less secretive than Stephen. No one at the company knew Stephen birded, not even Omar's wife. I only learned the truth when he pressed my wedding present into my hand: two-thousand-dollar binoculars.

What were we doing back of Interlaken that day, anyway? Stephen with a fishing hat, binoculars, camera equipment, a scope and a tripod on his back, me with a fishing hat, binoculars and a stadium kit, stalking around like thieves casing an entire landscape. Driving a huffing VW diesel up higher than you're allowed to go, driving through gates and across cattle guards to a private "alp" because birds like cars and hate people. Then back down with a whinchat, a shrike, two hawks and a chough, not much of a haul until we hit the species of least concern.

In December there was a cold snap, and Stephen came home in a state. "There's an evasion," he said. "We need to go north." All sorts of birds from far, far away that wintered in places like Denmark had decided even Holland was too cold, and were heading south in dribs and drabs, fetching up in swirling eddies near Zurich after they caught sight of the Alps.

"Oh, you go," I said. "I'm reading a book some guy raved about in the *Times* called *The Man Who Loved Children*."

"Sweetie," he said. He sat down next to me and put his arm around my shoulder. "I'm so sorry."

"No, no!" I said. "It's not like you're thinking. He has seven kids and he hates them. He's going to save the world with eugenics and euthanasia. I could go with you. But are you really sure I need to spend the weekend stumbling around on frozen dirt clods helping you level your tripod?"

"We could try again instead," he said. "Sex party weekend."

"I'm still kind of all tore up," I said. "You go."

"Twee," the wallcreeper remarked. "Twee!"

"Is it his suppertime?" I asked.

"It's only going to get worse," Stephen said. "Do you know what's happening to his gonads?"

"No."

"As his chin turns black, his testes are swelling from the size of pinheads to the looming, ponderous bulk of coffee beans."

"Wow," I said.

He kissed me. "His tiny heart is throbbing with love for someone he's never seen. I love you, too, you know." He embraced me, squeezing me very tight. "I love you so much, Tiffany." The wallcreeper protested. "Cool your jets, Rudolf," Stephen said.

He had named our bird after Rudolf Hess because its colors were those of a Nazi flag, with black on its chin for the SS in spring. To imply a certain tolerance for at least the form of his joke while rejecting its content, I had to suggest we name it after an anarcho-communist and came up, off the top of my head, with Buenaventura Durruti. But Rudolf stuck. So its name was Rudolf Durruti.

Sometimes I would sit and go over things Stephen had said during our whirlwind courtship, fitting them into a context I was learning only slowly. It was hard. He had told me so little about himself, intent on taking note of my little foibles so he could, for instance, surprise me with tickets to Berg's *Lulu*.

The birds were Stephen's intimate sphere. He didn't have to be cool or funny or even appetizing about them. "Breeding and feeding," Stephen called their lifestyle, making them sound like sex-obsessed gluttons (that is, human beings) instead of the light-as-air seasonal orgiasts they were in reality—ludicrously tragic animals, always fleeing the slightest hint of bad weather in a panic, yelling for months on end to defend territories the size of a handball court, having brief, nerdy sex and laying clutch after clutch of eggs for predators, taking helpless wrong turns that led them to freeze to death, drown, starve, or be cornered by hunters on frozen lakes, too tired to move.

To Stephen they were paragons of insatiable, elemental appetite. I saw them differently. I imagined two ducks, loyal partners. When the hunters cornered them, would they turn to face them, holding hands? Hell no. They would scatter like flies in as many directions as there were ducks. The duck who got hit would look up with his last strength to make eye contact with his lifelong friend, who would shake her head as if to say, "Hush now. Don't rat me out just because you're dying." Love would conquer all.

When my parents and my sister came for Christmas, I finally got out to see the old city. I took my parents to a craft market so Stephen could sleep with my sister. She worked as a bikini barista in greater Seattle and liked a good time. But he didn't sleep with her. She became irritable. She came into our bedroom with only panties on, asking to borrow my bathrobe. Stephen looked up for about a quarter of a second.

Berne was beautiful. It had colonnades like Bologna and boutiques like New York. On three sides of its grid, it fell away to a wild river in a gorge. The river enfolded the city like a uterine wall. Across the bridge bears stalked back and forth on the banks. It was too small to move through. All you could do was change positions in place. From the top of the church tower you could see all of it. Every speck. I went with my sister to cafés. She said she would marry Steve in a minute, but in Berne her eyes caressed everything and everyone. Everything in Berne had a delicious texture advertising a rich interior. Nothing was façade. It was clean all the way down forever and forever, like the earth in Whitman's "This Compost." I told Stephen I wanted to live there. He claimed in the old city you couldn't have a washing machine because the plumbing was medieval.

Our apartment was fifteen minutes from downtown Berne. Our trolley stop was next to a gas station, which is where Elvis the Montenegrin worked behind the counter, selling beer and candy. His shift ended around the time Stephen went to work. I bought the *International Herald Tribune* every day.

Pretty soon Elvis knew I spoke English. Soon after that he knew what baked goods I liked and how I liked my coffee. He knew how to smile charmingly and ask for sex by name. The first time I invited Elvis to our apartment, I realized that even the hottest hot sex with Stephen had been all in my head. I had hypnotized myself because Stephen had a job that could support us both and secretarial work bored me. I saw that I had followed the chief guiding principle of the petty bourgeoisie in modernity and made a virtue of necessity in telling myself my husband was a good lover. Elvis raised my consciousness. But there are reasons they call it necessity, so I decided Stephen's stability was good for me. Elvis was flighty. He had tight pants and a degree in superannuated theory from Ljubljana. He was always broke a week before payday. "I take what I want," he liked to say. He was hopelessly in love with his own thoughts, watching them like a show on TV, zapping through the channels. But he trusted his eyes, which was nice. He would absent-mindedly taste my sweat, or try the weight and flexibility of my hair, comparing it to heavy gold as if he had pulled off the heist of the century. My eyes struck him as particularly expensive. Objectifying my body saved him from objectifying my mind. He moved gracefully through and around me like a wave. My thoughts were my business. I thought, Elvis is a good lover.

Stephen unexpectedly announced that he had been to a music shop and acquired two telephone numbers. "I'm an operator," he explained. Even his taste in music was news to me. When I met him, his things were already in storage, and by the time the container with his vinyl collection arrived from Rotterdam, I was in the hospital. "Why, why, why do the wicked ones rule," he sang suddenly. He joined a sound system where everyone was younger than he was. I thought maybe something about his narrow escape from fatherhood had inspired him to become younger. He grew his hair an extra half-inch and started drinking energy drinks. He used headphones because his music might upset Rudolf, who was molting. I never had to go to their shows. Stephen said he needed his space, because we were going to be together for sixty-plus years.

So his knob-twiddling was the first thing I found out about Stephen other than myself and birds. The birds were secret from his coworkers, but they were all I got.

In March, Rudolf became very restless. He would climb his pegboards up to the crown molding, let go and drop to the floor, then flutter from room to room like an autumn leaf tied to a string. He stopped saying twee-twee-twee and started cheeping like a sparrow and crying out in delirium like a skylark. Stephen said Rudolf wanted to find a nesting site and sing himself a girlfriend. He definitely seemed very driven. One Sunday morning at dawn (we were going to Lake Biel) we opened the kitchen window for him. Rudolf flew out, then back. He clung to the stucco outside and looked at me. Stephen said, "Go on, Rudolf. This is Switzerland. You're safe!" Rudolf climbed straight up in short bursts of fluttering and was borne away on the wind. Stephen told me we should try again to have a baby, right now.

"What about zero population growth?" I objected.

"My mother and father were only children," he said. "That means I'm entitled to four to replace my grandparents."

"What about global warming?"

"If it weren't for global warming, we'd be under an ice sheet a mile thick right now." He gestured toward the mountains. "But look at us. Earth as far as the eye can see. I love global warming! And I love you!"

Something about the implied comparison made me nervous. I was pretty bad as wives go. Where Stephen was concerned possibly epoch-rending, world-destroying bad. But without me he'd be under an ice sheet, so maybe I was doing him a favor.

It was plausible. It was also not enough. I said I wasn't ready. But I had sex with him, feeling like a very dutiful wife.

Soon after that I went out to dinner downtown with Elvis. It was the day after payday. He talked nonsense and made me laugh. We walked the colonnades and fetched up against the ramparts, facing in. You couldn't look across the river. There was nothing there. Berne lived turned inward on itself. But it wasn't self-sufficient; it was more like a tumor with blood vessels to supply everything it needed: capital, expats, immigrants, stone, cement, paper, ink, clay, paint. No, not a tumor. A flower with roots stretching to the horizon, sucking in nutrients, but not just a single flower: a bed of mixed perennials. A flower meadow where butterflies could lay eggs and die in peace, knowing their caterpillars would not be ground to pulp by the mowers. Continuity of an aesthetic that had become an aesthetic of continuity. That was Berne. I leaned against the city wall and Elvis kissed me, closing his eyes so as not to see the bears. It was dark and freezing cold.

Birding in winter involves a lot of long car rides. (I saw Elvis a lot, so I didn't mind spending time with Stephen on weekends.) One morning I got around to begging Stephen to tell me about himself. He turned out to be much better at talking when he was driving the car. The landmarks steadily passing by the side of the road functioned as encouraging responses, telling him to go on. The distractions filled all the little gaps with what seemed like conjunctions linking dependent clauses. "You know, there's not much to say," he said. "I mean, I'm going to have to drop out of this sound system because they want to go on tour. I'm trying to think when I started playing drums. I guess maybe sixth grade. My parents got me lessons. I had a trap set in the basement. A red Tama drum kit. Getting lessons helps. Guys play for ten years and can't even do a snare roll if they never got lessons. My first band was Gold Purple Scarlet. We played this monumental Lovecraftian dark epic schlock," he smiled, borne away like a boat against the current, "and we looked like hobbit vampires. I had long hair and I was so into drugs. Prescription painkillers. Our lyrics were like 'Fear the vengeance of the blood dwarf, the moonlit trumpets ride,' shit like that. It was white supremacist, among other things. I mean, you don't know when you're a kid railing against hip-hop and the backbeat whose hands you're playing into. Whose freak flag, you know. My parents were in hell. Plus I was addicted to Darvon and sometimes codeine. But we had such a great time. It was like nothing existed outside of the band. We brought out an EP and two CDs, and then we broke up because Lydia, she was the singer, her parents got her put in the hospital, and when she got out, she was gone. She went up to Maine, like as far away as she could possibly get. She was walking silly walks from all the Prolixin. That's when I decided to go to med school and be a psychiatrist. But I had this problem of shitty grades and mediocre scores, so I went to that work-study program at Temple instead. I know devices are cool and everything like that, but I wish I'd had the patience for chemistry. I was so fucking lazy. I could be working on cancer or HIV, and here I am making parts for alcoholic smokers. So it's good I'm still doing music. And I have the cutest wife. Hardcore was never my thing when I was coming up. I was basically into anything where you wear black, the whole range from EBM to minimal techno. I was a lonely kid. My mom was such a weirdo, like a scarlet macaw. She was always wearing scarves and big pants, like 'flowing garments.' Did I ever tell you she slept with Paul from Peter, Paul and Mary? I would basically listen to absolutely anything where you got to wear black." He paused to make a left turn. "I kind of liked dub, you know, Lee Perry and Mad Professor and even goofy shit like Judge Dread, and I was really into Bootsy, plus like sludge and death metal, so that whole tight-ass rude-boy mod thing was not my idea of good. I liked psychedelics, but there was nowhere to get them. I was I guess eighteen when I did rehab. My dad was so mad at me. I thought he was going to kill me. I seriously thought he was taking me down to the clinic because he no longer trusted himself not to kill my ass. But my parents were pretty sweet to me most of the time. So anyway, it was when I got older and kind of settled down that I started getting into these heinous happy party sounds. You can't be into downers and listen to dubstep. It's not doable."

"Wait, how did you get into birds?"

"Oh, that was basically my scout leader. He also coached track, so we saw each other all the time. He had a house on the Chickahominy next to a marsh. It was brackish water, smelled totally anaerobic, but it got a lot of crabs. That was like paradise. We used to go crabbing all day. We'd go fishing in the morning in the pond back of the cove, fry bluegills and bass for lunch, tie up their heads on some string and go out and stand in the river barefoot, pulling in blue crabs. Then we'd build a fire and get this great big pot and some Old Bay and put a hurting on those crabs. I didn't much get into birds until I was at least, I don't know, sixteen? I wasn't a kid anymore. It was when the other kids were getting into hunting, I guess, and I knew that was not for me. He was my math teacher, too, so he used to tell me about the special theory of relativity and everything like that. He liked clamming a lot, but I really hated clams. So my eagle scout project was to study the ospreys that were breeding and feeding in the cove."

"I thought you were addicted to codeine."

"Listen, man, I went to state running the mile. There are a lot of hours in the day when you're a kid."

I had to admit the truth of that statement. I replied, "The most ambitious thing I did at that age was let these girls pierce my ears."

"I would have done anything in the world I thought would piss my parents off," Stephen said. "Eagle scout was a conscious trade-off to keep my dad from killing me."

I realized that he was not like me at all. I only did things I felt strongly moved to do. As a child I consistently felt I had no options and was surprised by my parents' strong reactions to the entirely inevitable things I did. My life moved forward in ineluctable leaps. The only smart leap I had ever made, in their opinions, was marrying Stephen. It was what set me apart from my sister, since secretary and bikini barista are not really such different professions when you get right down to it. I mean, I've served plenty of coffee in my day.

"Were you in a band at Temple?" I asked.

"No. Once I moved out of my parents' house, I calmed down a lot. I just didn't like having people breathing down my neck."

That made sense. It would be a reason to marry some-one too shy to ask personal questions. It was also a way of saying: I wasn't doing drugs when you met me and I'm not doing drugs now, but if you breathe down my neck, I'll do drugs.

"Isn't it hard," I asked, "getting up so early in the morning on weekends after you worked all week? I mean, it's hard for me, and I'm just writing a screenplay." (I had intimated that I was a writer with industry connections so he wouldn't make me work.)

"Oh, I feel great," he said. "It's great getting out of the lab. I feel exhilarated. I feel like I can concentrate for hours. I feel on top of the world right now. This is a really good time for me." He reached out and clamped his hand lovingly on my leg. He was shaking.

When we got to the river, I helped him set up his blind. It was a bit cramped, so first he would get in, and then I would hand him everything he needed before going back to the car to read.

He saw a greenshank, linnets, and a poacher. He made me look at the guy. We took a picture through his spotting scope, but it didn't turn out.

It was soon after that that I started saying, if he asked me what I was doing, "Oh, breeding and feeding." The majestic simplicity. It always made him laugh. But I couldn't envy the birds. Their lives weren't as simple as mine. My life was like falling off a log comfortably located somewhere light years above the earth.

*

At Elvis's suggestion I took a course in Berndeutsch. I learned ten verbs for work: work hard (*drylige, bugle, chrampfe, schaffe, wärche*), get stuck with jobs no one else wants to do (*chrüpple*), work slowly (*chnorze*), work carelessly (*fuuschte*), work absent-mindedly (*lauere*). Stay at home and putter around doing little harmless chores (*chlütterle*). I learned fast and the teacher said maybe it was an advantage my not knowing any German. Then the ten weeks of the course were over and I didn't know anything anymore, except that I would never look for a job. When people other than Stephen asked me what I did, I could say, "*Chlütterle*." Another laugh line.

Elvis said he wanted to go dancing, which would involve staying out very late. Going dancing was his reason for being, and he wanted to share it with me. I wasn't sure I could get that past Stephen, but I agreed to try. Stephen said, "That sounds like a date."

"It totally is a date. Obviously this guy wants in my pants. But I mean, when's the last time you went dancing? For me I think it was my sophomore year. And I wouldn't know where to go. He's a nice guy. I'm sure you know him. The guy with the beard at the gas station. He's totally harmless. He's a disciple of Slavoj Žižek."

Stephen snapped the *International Herald Tribune* tight to turn the page. "That is the tiredest line in Christendom," he said.

"I know. It's not his fault he's a tragic figure. It's never a tragic figure's fault. That's what makes them tragic. But he says he knows this really fun place to go dancing, not a disco but, like, a bar where they play all kind of 'mixed music.'"

"Do you need a chaperone?"

"Would you please?" I said. I couldn't really say no. We picked Elvis up at his place. I had never been there. It was farther out of town, up at the edge of the woods. An old house. He came out as soon as the car pulled up. The street obviously didn't get much traffic late at night. Elvis directed us to the most pitiful bar I ever saw. Young men unlikely to be in the possession of Swiss passports danced with eyes half-closed, snapping their fingers, while women in various states of disrepair jockeyed into their axes of attention. Lumpy, lantern-jawed, pockmarked, bucktoothed, short, tall, or simply drunken women, here to pick up devil-may-care subaltern gigolos for a night of horror.

I saw Elvis through new eyes. "You are so much beautiful," he would often say charmingly as he worshipped at the altar of my body. Looking around, I could only think that a bar where I am the best-looking woman by a factor of ten is not a bar where I want to be, and that beauty is apparently relative. I felt both better- and worse-looking than before. Better because I was suddenly reminded that the world is not all college girls and secretaries and trophy wives, and worse because everything in the whole universe is contagious if you look at it long enough. Just opening your eyes puts you in front of a mirror, psychologically speaking. Garbage in, garbage out. Or rather, garbage goes in, but you never get rid of it. It just lies there turning to dust and slowly wafting a thin layer of grime on to every other object in your brain. Scraping the gunk off is not only a major challenge, but the chief burden of human existence. That's why I keep things so clean. Otherwise I would see little flecks of Rudolf-shit everywhere I looked, from Fragonard to the *Duino Elegies*.

"I am not staying here," Stephen said. "Do you want to stay?"

Elvis asked if he knew another place. Our next stop was called Mancuso's Loft. It was running drum 'n' bass. The proprietor waved us in. Here I saw Stephen through new eyes. Then I ran to the ladies' room and stuffed my ears with toilet paper. Stephen led me to the floor and yelled, "I'm going to dance a little bit!" He then proceeded to dance as if he had never seen me, or any other human being, before in his life. Cranes came to mind.

Touching my elbow, Elvis remarked, "This club is so much beautiful," and headed for the bar. Elvis was right. In Mancuso's Loft, I felt below average-looking and quite conspicuously ill-dressed. My pants revealed nothing whatever. My shoes were comfy. My shirt had long sleeves so thick I was soon terribly hot.

"I like your husband," Elvis said. I said that was not really his assigned task. "No, he has something. Un certain je ne sais quoi. You know what I need? A girlfriend. By myself, I am never getting into this place. You think they let me in? A brown man alone, with a beard? Ha!"

"You're not brown! You're lily-white anywhere but Denmark!"

"Many times, I am standing in the queue outside clubs like this. And all the time, I think I am living in Berne. But I am not living in Berne. I am living in the Berne that reveals itself to me, okay, a white 'Yugo' if you please but with no connections, with nothing. A cashier in the petrol station, with nothing to his account but a few women. Yes, I say it openly. I have nothing to offer this town but my body. My body to strike the keys of the cash register, my body to find other bodies and search for warmth. My body is my capital. You, this beautiful woman, are my social capital. And then I was taking you, you particularly, to this horrible bar. I see now it is so very horrible, this bar."

"Elvis, calm down," I said. "You're a model of successful integration. You even speak Berndeutsch, and you've only been here eleven years!"

"Are they speaking Berndeutsch in this club? No, they speak French!" I didn't know how he had decided on that one, because I could barely hear even him, much less other people. "I speak the language of the gas station! I have shamed myself. I hoped to leverage one woman to meet another. Not to earn a woman with the honest work and the natural beauty of my body! This crazy Swiss language has made me a capitalist of women! And what is my wages? I insult you, the most beautiful woman in Switzerland. This town has made of me a body without a brain. I will leave this place and go to Geneva," he concluded, taking both my hands.

"Don't do that," I said.

"No, I won't if you don't permit it!" he cried ecstatically, throwing his arms around me.

Stephen drifted over, bouncing on the tips of his toes, and beckoned to me. "You need ketamine?" he whispered.

"Umm, no?" I said.

"I got three," he said. "I think I might stay here. You want the car keys? I'll take a taxi."

"Don't give Elvis any drugs."

"I don't take drugs," Elvis volunteered. He had never been in a band, so he could hear much better than we could. Stephen and I were always stage-whispering about people sitting near us in cafés and drawing stares.

"That's dandy," I said. I pocketed the keys and took Elvis's hand. "Let's blow this joint. That okay with you?"

Stephen mouthed the word, "Arrivederci."

We arrived at the wind-struck farmhouse where Elvis lived with (judging from angle of the stairs) a herd of chamois and mounted to the third floor hand in hand. After a warm and harmonious session of sixty-nine (Elvis was not too tall) to the sounds of Montenegrin folk rock (East Elysium—my favorite song was "Wings [Who You Are?]"), he said, "I want to buttfuck you."

"What is it with guys?" I said. "You're all obsessed."

"I never mentioned it before!"

"So where did you get the idea? From bad porn with stock footage from the sixties? From daring postmodern novels like *Lady Chatterley's Lover*?"

"From doing it."

"FYI, it's no fun, so forget it."

"Just forget it?"

"Forget it."

Elvis said mournfully, "If you loved me, you wouldn't care that it's 'no fun.' That's the difference between our thing and a real love."

"Wait a second," I said. "I don't mean to sound like a crank, but are you saying that what makes our relationship valuable is my willingness to suffer for you? Are you aware that I've never suffered for you for even, like, one second? That's what makes our relationship so optimal, in my opinion."

"You must have done buttfucking to know that it's 'no fun.' So you suffered for someone else, right?"

"So now you want to move up in the world?"

"I'm in love with you. I want a sign that I mean so much to you."

"You asked me if I'd move to Geneva with you, and I said no. You accepted that right away."

"I can't ask so much of you. That's too much."

"Are you aware that if you gave me a choice, like if I actually had two options in life, anal sex and moving to Geneva—"

"You would move to Geneva?" He threw his arms around me again, quivering with spontaneous joy.

"You're not understanding me," I said, pushing pillows in the corner so I could sit up. "There's suffering, and then there's boring stuff, and then there's stuff that's just plain stupid. I've done my share of suffering for Stephen. And other guys. Like crucifixion, I mean that level of suffering. Like St. Laurence. 'Turn me over! I'm done on this side!' I don't see what that has to do with having a good relationship. It should be about getting through difficult stuff together. Difficult stuff the world throws at you, not difficult stuff you do to each other. The difference right now between me and St. Laurence is, he didn't have the option of taking his hand off the hot stove."

"You are fierce," he replied, pulling the blanket up around his naked body to hide it. "I am never asking another woman for buttfucking."

"Are you bisexual?"

He frowned. "I am polymorphous pervert! Where I find love!"

I shifted back into neutral and once again accepted the need for negative capability in this world. We had loving, beautiful sex just as soon as we could get ourselves to stop talking—loving and beautiful in the expressionist, pathetic-fallacy sense in which you might say a meadow was loving and beautiful even if it was full of hamsters ready to kill each other on sight, but only when they're awake. I mean, you just ignore the hamsters and look at the big picture.

The next day, around six p.m. after he woke up, Stephen said, "Let's make a baby."

"I feel like Saint Laurence on the gridiron," I said.

"No, you're mixed up. Miscarriage is nothing compared to childbirth. You got off easy. You're like Saint Laurence saying he doesn't want to go to Italy in July. I'm asking

you right now to risk your life and health for my reproductive success. I feed, you breed. Come on!"

"Sounds tempting," I said. "If I could lay eggs and you
agreed to sit on them, I might even do it."

"Can we fake it?" he said. "Are you fertile?"

"Not exactly."

"Then meet the father of your triplets!"

"You're totally insane," I said approvingly. Stephen was
actually sort of interesting when his mind opened the
iron gates a crack and let the light out.

"The central ruling principle of my life," Stephen
explained in a grandfatherly way, "is 'Let's Not And Say
We Did.' Most people don't give a fuck what you've done
and not done. If I put a picture of you and a baby on my
desk, I can get promoted. All anybody wants to know is
little sketchy bits of information, strictly censored, and
that's enough. It's more than enough. Did you ever sit
down and actually make a list of what you know about,
like, Togo? 'Is in Africa.' That would be the grand total of
your knowledge. But when people say the word 'Togo'
you let it pass, the same way you let hundreds of people
pass you on the street and in the halls every day. And
every one of them is as big as Togo, inside."

"That's pure bathos, and I know nothing about Togo," I
said. "But somebody like, say, Omar's wife, I don't know
her either, but what with my life wisdom and mirror
neurons and all that, I figure I have a pretty good sense of
what she's about. But only because I've met her. I mean,
if I said, 'Togo is charming,' you'd get the idea that you
liked it until further notice, but if then I said, 'Togo brags

about doing those impossible word puzzle things in the *Atlantic* and dropping out of Harvard med to get a doctorate in nutrition,' you'd think, who is it trying to impress? But you haven't even begun to talk about its secret sorrows or whatever."

"You can bet your buttons Togo has secret sorrows," Stephen said. "If anybody knew what they were, the world would be filled with raw, bowel-torn howling. That's Stanislaw Lem. I was going to say, I didn't love you when I married you. It was like, 'Let's Not And Say We Did.' But now I feel like Apu in *The World of Apu*, except instead of being faithful to me and dying in childbirth like you're supposed to, you're fucking this Arab guy. So tell me, Tiff, *what is going on?*"

"He's Montenegrin!"

"Montenegrin my ass! He's Syrian if he's a day! 'Elvis'! It's like a Filipino telemarketer calling himself Aragorn!"

I pouted.

"Ever try to make a list of everything you know about Elvis?"

"What would be the point? I was just trying to have some exciting sex."

"Could you not try?"

I was silent.

"Could you love me a little?"

"Actually I do love you. Elvis told me. It's breaking his heart."

*

On Monday morning I bought the *International Herald Tribune* and some milk and said, "Elvis, I need to talk to you." For the first time I noticed that he was reading *Hürriyet*. Over coffee at my place, he explained that his family had left Montenegro some generations before. But their women preserved the legendary beauty and kindness of the people of Montenegro, once immortalized so memorably by Cervantes in his lady of Ulcinj (D'ulcinea), and their men weren't bad either. He showed me his Turkish passport. His name really was Elvis.

"Tiffany, my love," he said. "What does it matter where I am from? You are an American! You know better than any shit European that we are all equal children of God!"

The next Saturday we went birding to an ugly artificial lake and Stephen asked me to talk about myself. "Let's see," I said, "being little sucked, but it had its advantages. Sledding is a lot more exciting before you turn ten. Of course I couldn't really swim until I was eleven."

"And then?"

"Well, my parents weren't real particular about their choice of a boarding school, so I went to basically a home for wayward girls. I didn't learn a whole lot. Like, our chemistry teacher was the choir director's wife. I used to play around in the lab on weekends. I used to dump all the mercury on the counter and play with it."

"Yeah?"

"I was supposed to go to Bryn Mawr after my junior year, but it was too much money, so I took a scholarship to Agnes Scott."

He shuddered appreciatively.

"Then I moved to Philly and got a job, and then I met you."

"Short life."

"Well, life is short."

"My child bride."

"Hey, it's not that bad! I had a thing with the riding coach at school, and in Philly I OD'd on heroin and they called me crusty mattress-back!"

"What?"

"I'm kidding. That was somebody else. This girl name of, um, Cindy——"

"You just made her up."

"Okay, her name was Candy. I'm serious. Candy Hart. It sounds like a transvestite from Andy Warhol's factory, so probably she made it up. She said she was from Blue Bell, so probably she was from Lancaster, and she said she was fourteen, so probably she was seventeen. I've never met anybody I can be entirely sure I've actually met."

We saw bearded reedlings and a ruff. We would have seen more, but there were dog walkers there scaring everything off.

We went on a birding vacation to the lagoons of Bardawil. All the men I saw there reminded me of Elvis.

When I got back I demanded answers. He cradled his coffee in his hands and said, "Now I am telling you the truth. I am a Syrian Jew. My grandfather converted to Catholicism in 1948, but he took a Druze name by mistake and was not trusted by the Forces Libanaises, so then——"

"Just shut up," I said. "I think you're cute. That's your nationality. Cute."

On the phone my sister said, "Tiff, you have got to get a life. You think I have time to have sex? Guess again! I spend so much money on outfits for work I had to get another job!"

I said to Stephen at dinner that maybe we should try again to have a child. Our marriage had begun in the most daunting way imaginable. We had barely known each other, and then we had those accidents and that jarring disconnect between causes (empty-headed young people liking each other, wallcreepers) and effects (pain, death).

He objected. He said, "I'm sure there are couples that are fated to be together, like they meet each other in kindergarten and date on and off for twenty years, and finally they give up because they realize they've gotten so far down their common road that there's nobody else in the entire universe they can talk to, because they have a private language and everything like that. Do you really think that applies to us? What do we have in common? We don't even have Rudi anymore."

"A baby would be something in common."

"That's it. Have kids and turn so weird from the stress that nobody else ever understands another word we say. A couple that's completely wrapped up in each other can get through anything, because they don't have a choice. Right now we have the option of floating through life without being chained to anybody, but instead we pile on a ton of bricks and go whomp down to the ground."

"Are we ever going to both want a baby at the same time?"

"I hope not!" Stephen said. "I want to float through life. I like being with you, and I don't want to be chained to anybody. I mean, when you got pregnant, I could deal, but if you're not pregnant, I can also deal."

"That's a relief. I was afraid if I didn't have kids soon, you'd make me get a job."

He paused and looked at me fixedly for a good ten seconds. "I'm starting to catch on to you," he said. "You were born wasted. You live in a naturally occurring K-hole."

"I do my best."

"Here's the deal. I need your baby for my life list. It's one of the ten thousand things I need to do before I die, along with climbing Mt. Everest and seeing the pink and white terraces of Rotomahana. The baby is the ultimate mega-tick."

"Like a moa," I suggested.

"Exactly. There will never be another one like it, and there was never one like it ever, so actually it's a moa that arose from spontaneous generation. A quantum moa."

"Babies are totally quantum," I said. "That's why it feels so weird when they die. You feel like it had its whole entire life taken away and all the lights went out at once, like it got raptured out of its first tooth and high school graduation in the same moment."

We munched on food for a bit.

I said, "Stephen, may I ask you something? When we had anal sex that one time, was that for your life list?"

"Yeah."

"It wasn't on my list."

"I'm sorry. I figured human beings are curious. I try not to avert my eyes when life throws new experiences my way. But I guess nobody ever asked me to stick the pelagics up my ass."

At nine o'clock on a November morning I looked out the kitchen window and saw three birders on the sidewalk digiscoping me. When I opened the curtain, they moved their hands frantically from side to side at waist level, as if to say, Stop! When I opened the window, they shouted, "Halt! *Nicht bewegen!*" I stuck my head out and looked around. Rudolf was waiting under the eaves. When he saw me, he let go, dropped two stories, and then fluttered up and in.

Stephen was overjoyed for a day and a night. Then I was on all the birding forums as wallcreeper girl. People were writing embarrassing things. They wrote, "*Bernerin ist gut zu Vögeln*," the oldest joke in the book. Bernese woman is nice to birds/Bernese woman is a good fuck.

You could call it homonyms or a pun, but actually the only difference is that the birds are capitalized.

Birders are sort of a male version of the women in that bar Elvis took us to. They attract birds by kissing their thumbs until it squeaks. They can't exactly attract women that way, but why would they want to? Women are ubiquitous, invasive—the same subspecies from the Palearctic to Oceania. Trash birds. However, it should be noted, birders are primates and thus, like birds, respond to visual cues. I had leaned out the window in a loose bathrobe, first drawing my hair to one side around the back of my neck so it wouldn't get in the way. Everybody likes a woman barefoot in breeding plumage in the kitchen. Stephen said if ornitho.ch had a habit of publishing the locations of wallcreeper sightings we would be in deep shit, and also that I should get a modeling contract for optics like Pamela Anderson for Labatt's.

Whenever I looked at the video online, I saw Elvis standing faintly illuminated in the deep shadow of the kitchen. But Stephen only had eyes for Rudolf and his floppy rag-doll trajectory up his spiral staircase of air into my arms. Stephen really did love birds. Plus psychedelic drugs, discretion, and sarcasm. The beard kept Elvis from having a face-shaped face. His dark body hair broke up the outline of his naked torso like camouflage on a warship.

As I screwed Rudolf's bacon into his pegboards with my thumb I felt glad we were too poor to live downtown. Rudolf would never have found us. Would he?

Rudolf sang, "Toodle-oodle-oo!"

*

Stephen and I loved nature more than ever after we'd decided to ignore its effects in our own lives. We chose to love it instead of bending under its weight. If you're out in a swamp every weekend morning, you're not breeding and feeding. You're in control. You need to stay out of nature's way while you're still young enough for it to ruin your life.

Or maybe I just thought that way because Stephen's father had a pacemaker and it was the bane of his existence. That's what he told me that day down on the dock: that he would die when the goddamn battery finally ran the hell down. In the private language shared by the extended family of western civilization, it had become impossible to connect nature and death. Nature was the locus of eternal recurrence, the seasons like coiled springs, the Lion King taking his father's throne, the inexorable force of life that floods in and covers Surtsey with giraffes and hoopoes. Where it is apparent that there is no death, human beings are planed down to fear of failing technology: the loose seat belt that ratcheted too late and walloped Tiff, Jr. upside the head, the pricey polyurethane condom that was supposed to be so great and created her in the first place. We failed technology when it needed us most. The beaches were disappearing not because the oceans were rising, but because we hadn't built the right walls to keep them out. We needed storm cellars and snow tires and environmentally friendly air conditioning. I needed to get to thirty-five without having a baby and then blame IVF. And meanwhile, nature itself was dying, one life at a time.

After two years in Berne, Stephen was still working on two migratory ducks. Two pretty common ducks actually, so it was a mystery why he didn't have them yet. We would go out every Sunday morning to one little body of water or another and see everything but these damn ducks. He desperately, in his opinion, needed someone reliable to tell him where to find the ducks. So at long last he joined the Swiss Society for the Protection of Birds. He started entering his backlog of observations on ornitho.ch instead of just lurking. Four weekends in a row he went out with one of them instead of me. He didn't make any mistakes.

They had a thing for English speakers. England is the mythical Eden where every rude mechanical knows what is nesting where in his garden and woodcocks eat out of your hand, and America is the land of the citizen scientist and the bag limit. American hunters shoot five ducks in the first five minutes of the season and rest on their laurels. Models of reason and restraint.

So they trusted Stephen, even though birders under fifty were reportable to the Swiss Rarities Committee. Stephen knew his birds. They gave him a piece of protected marsh to count birds in, every Sunday in winter and once a month in summer. They promised him his ducks had an excellent chance of turning up. So he sat there behind his spotting scope looking at mallards until about mid-January and then decided maybe something was wrong with Sundays. He tried Saturday and saw about two thousand birds—various rails, fudge ducks, tufted ducks, common pochards (female), red-crested pochards, and a juvenile eagle.

The next morning he asked me to come with him. He wanted to take off at five o'clock. I forced myself. We didn't have to look long for the guy. We heard him. He was hunting from a boat on the other side of the creek.

"No way!" Stephen said. We could sort of make him out dragging the boat up into the reeds, and heard him call his dog and start his car. It was Sunday, with no birds anywhere in sight except the ultimate in trash—those sinister little chickadees everybody feeds, who hang around all winter and get dibs on the nesting sites the good birds need. Luckily ninety percent of them die anyway of hunger and cold.

"It's a crime against nature!" Stephen said, frowning.

I pointed out that the trend in recent jurisprudence has been to broaden the scope of so-called crimes against humanity and subsume all other offenses under them. He didn't listen.

His first idea for a solution did not bode well. He wanted to buy a .22. His next idea was to spend a lot of money on video equipment. His third idea was to talk to the Society for the Protection of Birds, who said you can't have everything. Hunting is way below what it used to be. Actually it's down to almost nothing in Switzerland. It's the peaceable kingdom. Seriously. The red-crested pochards come there from Spain, north for the winter.

*

The beautiful Elvis bred and fed. He rang our doorbell with Kaiser rolls and a hangdog expression and said, "Oh, Tiff, it is so much terrible. My ex-wife is pregnant. I will become a father. She will not get an abortion."

"Don't tell me," I said. "I literally don't care." That was not true at all, but I had learned to draw back at the sight of the forces of nature. "Either you want to continue our relationship," I continued, "or you don't. But don't just come in here and tell me something like that without putting it into context. By context I mean direct relevance for me personally. A purely pragmatic context, like are you never coming over here again, or will you be coming less often, or you can come for the next six months and that's it. Give me your findings and skip the data."

"But that's not it," he said. "I will take custody of this baby. I will care for it, nurse it. I will receive a minimum of social help money and I will stop working at the petrol station. But I cannot stay living in this rat-hole. I will move to a new house."

"What ex-wife? You could start by explaining what ex-wife you're talking about."

"My second wife, Alexandra in Geneva."

"Oh, Elvis," I said. "You're literally driving me insane."

I covered my eyes with my hands and thought: Back when I met Elvis it took me one look to know this guy gets into scrapes. I just didn't know what kind of scrapes, beyond sleeping with me because I was female. When I met Stephen, on the other hand, it was obvious that we were the same sub-subspecies of control freak. Even my parents saw it. Stephen has a fair level of control, and he figures at some point I'll get control and stop spending all my time compulsively coming up with ways to excuse my lack of it. He has those seven habits of highly effective people, and he's graciously letting me pick up one habit at a time. Elvis, though; I can't even tell whether Elvis is asking me for money. "Are you asking me for money?" I asked.

I didn't tell Stephen I had broken up with Elvis, because I wasn't really sure he didn't think it had been over a while ago. So I kept quiet and signed up for a German course. High German. A language with actual books. I was tired of *chlütterle*. I had to do something, because the minute I broke up with Elvis, I fell in love with him. I loved Stephen's disinformation dumps, but they wore me out. I missed Elvis's scattershot stupidity. It had been like a dalliance with a sixteen-year-old shepherdess, and my marriage was starting to feel like an exercise in opportunity cost.

I knew from reading *The Joy Luck Club* at the tearful insistence of my mother that sex is legal tender for all debts public and private, while husbands should be exploited to the max and beyond, but without Elvis coming over anymore, I couldn't even sit in my bed and read without being overwhelmed by memories. I couldn't even call them memories. Actually I was painfully turned on. I felt like a cat in heat with hallucinations. I thought, Wow, love is as strong as death! I never understood that before, and now I know it! And all because I—as in me, personally, of my own accord—ordered Elvis to stop coming around. I felt like generations of bluesmen whining about women they shot to death.

Then I realized that if I was looking for a sixteen-year-old shepherdess, I didn't have to look farther than my own black, jagged heart, and I picked myself up and went to class.

Word of Rudi's location spread like a slow fire in a coal seam. Birders called confidentially and conspiratorially to get permission to come by. After a while he was pretty much trained. I would put him on the crown molding and he would drop and fly back up while cameras whirred and lenses purred, each worth more than our car. A feature appeared in *Gefiederte Welt*. I had been afraid of turning into a poster child, but once they saw Rudi, no one looked at me anymore. Long before it was time for him to leave for the mountains, there were voices calling for a GPS transponder. Stephen and I liked the idea. We could go visit him in summer, assuming he wasn't hanging around in some inaccessible chasm. Maybe meet his family! Or at least see him collect nesting material. The transponders they have now are little tiny things, no more burden than, say, a quarter in my pocket would be for me. That's what they told us, and it sounded plausible enough. It would increase his body weight, but given how much better he ate than most wallcreepers in winter, he ought to be able to handle the strain.

Stephen had undergone a subtle but perceptible emotional shift from thinking of the wallcreeper as *Tichodroma muraria* to thinking of him as our unique and irreplaceable friend Rudi. You might think now would have been a good time to build him an aviary and buy bird toys. But his coal-black chin, his restlessness, that cease-less shrieking—his tiny sex drive was reducing him to a gemlike flame. Our instincts were sufficient to find him attractive, delightful, and guilt-inducing, but not sexy. He had to go away. But not entirely away. That was our plan. The ornithologist gave him three colored bands and a chip on the small of his back.

One Saturday we found him. Stephen drove almost to the edge of a chasm, set up the scope, and scanned the rock wall below us. Finally he said, "There's Rudi. Hey, Rudi! Hey, he's got a nest! Way to go, Rudi! Check him out. He's hiding. Mother fuck!"

I got my binoculars focused on Rudi in time to see the tiny hawk raise his head wet to the nostrils with Rudi's blood and plunge it again into Rudi's chest. Rudi's beautiful red and black wings with their absurd white polka dots twitched, twitched again, and died. The hawk ate his heart and flew away.

Stephen sat down and hyperventilated. Rudi's wife hopped once and flicked her wings. Then she, too, flew away. I suspected her of leaving nestlings to die because she was too damn lazy to raise them alone. "Fucking bitch," I said.

"I hope that motherfucking bastard dies," Stephen said. "If I had a gun I would shoot every motherfucking sparrowhawk in the whole goddamn Alps."

When Rudi died, Stephen stopped raising his eyes above the horizontal. He stopped going out at night or to the marsh. He read every word of the newspaper, offering lengthy, cogent commentary on the financial news as if he had been asked to join the president's council of economic advisers. He enlightened me on the relations between oil-producing and -consuming states as if he were grooming me for a position on his staff. His personal interests were subrogated to those of the mass media, and he began to seem like a nearly normal person. He stopped shaking. He never got excited. When he went to bed his face turned into a slack, unhappy mask and he never looked at me before he closed his eyes.

Stephen's grief humanized him. I began to fall in love.

While Stephen was out on Saturday morning buying ingredients for a salad, Omar's wife appeared at our door excited and trembling. She blew her nose and told me Omar had applied for a transfer to Topeka and she couldn't imagine life without us. "Now I'm sorry I never touched your red-hot husband," she said, flopping down on the couch.

It was clear that she meant to imply that her failure to seduce Stephen created a major obligation on my part.

She could easily have taken him, who was my sole and only meal ticket as far as anybody could tell, but she hadn't and now I owed her one.

"I didn't realize how much you meant to me until Omar's news came through," she said. "My heart just tore in little pieces. I couldn't figure out why. I felt so forlorn and disoriented. I ended up walking around until I was standing under Stephen's window at the lab, just hoping to see him. That's when I realized you're the only people I care about in this town. I'm going to miss you both so much!"

Stephen's lab was a solid car ride away and his office was on the ground floor of a modernist R&D-campus building that overlooked a compensatory wetland like an amphitheater, so what she said made no particular sense. She had probably tried to get his attention through the window because she couldn't get past the security at the doors in her jogging outfit, and probably eight hundred guys saw her, and so much for Stephen's plan of professional advancement via the chi of an irreproachable family life. Maybe they had been sleeping together, before Rudi died and Stephen withdrew from everything and everybody? Or did it make more sense if they had been doing it afterwards? Stephen had been very distant.

"That's a shame," I said. "I can't speak for myself, but Stephen's definitely a very special guy. It's sweet of you to think you'll miss us."

"Oh, Tiff. The truth is, Stephen means the world to me."

I shook my head.

"Don't worry," she added. "It's unrequited love. I don't think he knows I'm alive."

I shook my head again, mostly because I couldn't imagine an adult woman claiming to be in love without having slept with the guy first. But you never know. Maybe she was the kind who feels guilty when she commits adultery in her heart?

"Omar is a wonderful man," she explained. "But you know how sometimes one person can, what I mean is, I think my relationship with Omar was working mostly because Stephen was giving me something Omar just can't give me. I mean Stephen's way of talking, that sort of wild side he has. Omar's a very conventional guy. Sometimes I feel like he's kind of two-dimensional." She stumbled along, obviously unused to explaining her actions or motivations to anyone and therefore making them as transparent as frog spawn. She wasn't up to prevaricating with every word, the skill she so admired in Stephen. It takes a lifetime of practice. She had found her master, her teacher, too late. She simply knew she was about to lose something valuable, and like anybody else, she wanted to take the next logical step to make it her own: She wanted to fuck it.

I more or less stopped listening and filled in for her. Stephen, I thought to myself, is like a comet in near-earth orbit whose magnificent tail, streaming in the solar wind, defies long-standing questions regarding its ultimate composition, and compared to him Omar doesn't even seem quite human—I mean in the classical sense of being made in the image of a god or God—whereas Stephen possesses the indefinable divine spark that arises from friction between an infinitely complex universe and the unfathomable enigma of subjectivity, plus Omar is compulsive and getting seriously chubby from all the overtime he does. According to Stephen, he basically lives in the lab.

"I have a big crush on Stephen," I said. "I can see where you like him. But I bet there are plenty of cool guys in Topeka. I mean, out there they don't have any choice! People in Topeka can't stumble around like culture zombies following all the latest trends. They have to get creative. You're going to like the Midwest, I swear. There's more real art going on in one square inch of Midwest than in all of New York City. We'll come see you! Who knows, maybe Stephen will end up getting transferred there, too. What's Omar working on?"

"The contraption. The regulatory environment is better in the U.S.," she said.

The contraption was somehow based on the stent, but I didn't know it had anything to do with animal health, or even what it was.

She told me, if not in so many words: "The female-to-male transsexual market is much more lucrative when it's not covered by health insurance. You know how the companies negotiate the prices down."

"Right," I said.

"And you can't do experimental surgery on higher primates in Switzerland. It's impossible. I mean, this place has a formal policy on the dignity of *plant* life!"

She wanted to be sardonic but conveyed only vain indignation. Incapacity for irony was another thing keeping her from coming across, where Stephen was concerned, as anything but horny.

"In Topeka they can probably get human volunteers," I said. "They're cheaper than pygmy chimps."

"In my opinion the transsexual indication is one big smoke-screen. The contraption is for everybody." She held my gaze steadily. "Once it has regulatory approval, it's going to be an off-label gold mine."

I realized she was offering me an insider stock tip. I asked her how far the contraption was down the pipeline.

"It's not even phase one, but it's two years to launch," she said. "It's accelerated because the application is so exotic nobody cares whether it's safe."

"It reminds me of, like, a Kurt Vonnegut story," I said. "No way it will sell to anybody in his right mind. I remember they tried to move Stephen to the contraption six months ago and he said no way."

"I wish Omar were as smart as Stephen," she sighed.

"Omar's going to have a way bigger career than Stephen," I assured her. "I mean, you already said this project has huge potential, right? And he's got a lead position, right? So where's he going to be coming off it? Looking pretty good! It's definitely a step up from the beagles. You can kick back and play tennis in Topeka for a couple years, then come back here with vice president Omar and live the life of Riley! Stephen will still be futzing around doing God knows what when you get back.

You're not going to miss anything. His amazing brain isn't going anywhere. He'll be fat and bald with a heart condition because he never gets any exercise except driving and eating tater tots" (tater tots, known as *Rösti*, are a staple of the Swiss diet), "but trust me, he'll be here."

"Look at me," she said. "I'm a woman." Irony was truly not her forte.

"Stephen's a stick-in-the-mud," I said. "He's heavy into inertia. It leaves him plenty of time to think, but it's not something I'd be idealizing if I were you."

"I just can't imagine not seeing him anymore."

"What I'm telling you is, Stephen is a creature of habit. He's not sexy. There are a billion sexier guys in Berne. Just go to any bar." I jumped up and put an end to the vulgarity of our conversation by moving toward the kitchen to get more coffee.

She raised her voice and said, "Omar is an amazing lover, by the way."

That did it. I came back jittery. "God! Jesus!" I said. "What do you want from me?"

"Do you know about the Swiss law on divorce?" she said. "If Omar fools around on me, even once, I can keep the apartment. And alimony! It's like the 1950s! I know you better than you think. Can you do this for me? I know Omar adores you. I know you'll say he's Stephen's best friend, but that just makes it worse, as in even better!"

"You're that scared of *Topeka*?" I said. "It's not the South Pole!"

"I can't survive another day with Omar. He's driving me crazy. I'm going insane with boredom. I'm so in love with Stephen, and you don't care about Stephen! Come on! It would mean so much to me to be able to stay in Berne."

"Hey, I like Berne, too," I said. "Plus I think Stephen likes me better than he likes you. As in, I'm not sure your odds are so great."

She scoffed.

"I've come to realize," I said, "that there's generally something special about the person you would marry. It's not like I ever married anybody else. But I married Stephen, and he married me. I still don't know why it seemed like the thing to do, but I don't regret it, and neither does he."

She got to her feet. "My blood is on your hands," she said. "I can't feel this trapped and survive. You don't love Stephen, and I do." Her hands were pressed against her heart and she was taking the feeling of emptiness there very, very seriously—a hole in her heart only Stephen's dick could fill.

"Lighten up," I said. "Marriage isn't a sacrament. It's just a bunch of forms to fill out. It either works or it doesn't. Do what you want. You're grown up, and Omar's a big boy. Get a job and stay in Berne! You'll have a new boyfriend in like four minutes. Look at you."

"But I want our apartment. Tiff, I *need* your *help*."

"Me sleeping with Omar won't give you Stephen," I said. "I don't think you'd have much chance with him anyway. He's weird."

"What do you mean? Is Stephen kinky?"

I didn't want to explain that he had delusions in which he had been chosen alone among men to live life to the fullest, so I said, "For one thing, he's bi."

A look of profound consternation flashed across her beautiful face, and I knew they had slept together without condoms.

I suggested to Stephen that we move downtown. If we had moved before, Rudi couldn't have found us again, but now Rudi was gone and we could move.

Stephen didn't answer. He said he'd been in touch with an Italian breeder. He rummaged through his messenger bag on the floor, produced a handwritten letter, sat down on the couch, and read aloud.

"About *Tichodroma*. I have had for thirty years always one pair, changing them every six years in good health. In March the male is strongly singing. The female is strongly seeking him. They are divided but one can see the other. *Tichodroma* never die except for special infective reason. But older they make worse thermoregulation. A false microclimate will very much compromise the reproduction. *Tichodroma* is an absolute vagrant, seeking always those sunny days with a light fresh wind. He is using different environments always. There is no place where to have *Tichodroma* all the year." He looked up and made eye contact.

Stephen had stooped so low as to punish me with a fable involving a cute dead friend. As he intended, I felt very, very guilty. I had assumed hurting husbands was a privilege of bad wives. Suddenly I realized it's a moral shortcoming of good ones—good in the way I felt at that moment, in the sense of making a doomed, feeble attempt to be good, which is as good as it gets in the Judeo-Christian tradition where the imagination of man is evil from his youth.

"Move downtown by yourself," he added. "I'll pay your rent."

"Does this have anything to do with Omar's wife?" I asked.

I surprised even myself. I said it the way I might castle out of spite at not knowing anything about chess, just to prove I was in over my head.

"That bitch?" he said. "I wouldn't fuck her for practice."

"Is that why she's in love with you?" I demanded. "Are you trying to tell me it's your beautiful mind? She told me you did the nasty and Omar can't get it up! And then she asked me to suck him off live on camera so she can get a Swiss divorce! It's true! If he's unfaithful to her she can totally clean him out, Joy-Luck-Club style!"

Stephen said, "Come over here so I can beat the shit out of you."

I took his hand and lay down beside him, turning over to nestle up against his chest as if he had a brood patch. We looked over in silence at the wall unit where Rudi used to flit in and out of a shoebox twenty times a minute.

With the easy air of someone who believes he is gratifying a lover's private obsession, Stephen confided in me that he didn't believe the Italian guy was really breeding wallcreepers. "I think he's selling birds he paid some climber to liberate. As in steal nestlings. You know some songbirds can be a real pain in the ass to breed. A lot of them are solitary except when they're breeding, and everything has to be totally right or they never get in the mood. If you put them together the wrong day they do like bird jujitsu. You know how Rudi was always flicking his wings? That's because it's so loud next to these alpine streams nobody can hear him yelling. He was using his wings to say 'Get off my property.' But if he says it too much, his whole camouflage is out the window. It's a fine line. It's hard, trying to defend your territory and advertise your presence and keep out of predators' line of sight. So I thought about it, and I thought, I don't think I want to take somebody's nestlings out of his nest, right when he finally found a cave he likes and somebody he can get along with. But the truth is, if you take their chicks, they just make more. They can lay thirty eggs a season. They're set up for it. I mean, the reason chickens keep laying eggs is because somebody takes them away."

"You want to get a pet wallcreeper to prove Rudi was a dime a dozen," I said. "That's cold!"

"That's not true," he said. "No wallcreeper is a dime a dozen. They're lovely birds."

"Like women," I said. "Same-same but different."

"Every woman is unique in her own way and most of them are pieces of shit. Whereas any wallcreeper is an avatar of the one true wallcreeper."

"Name of Rudi," I said.

He turned and lay on his back and said, "Fuck it. I mean it. We're all fucked. Saving one single wild thing was more than I could manage, which means the whole world is fucked. But then I remember that you know how to look out for yourself, and I feel better. Like it's not the weight of the world, just my own little column of air."

I was happy. He had called me a wild thing.

Our new apartment was weensy. It was on the former second floor (the street had risen over the years) of a tiny medieval house and, according to the commission on cultural monuments, too historic to renovate. Replacing everything that needed replacing would have meant tearing down the entire house by slow stages from the inside out, clod by clod and pebble by pebble. Its pristine construction elements, dangerous and pointless as they were from a fire safety standpoint, were irreplaceable: intricately woven willow lathes, soundproofing made of rye chaff. "Soundproofing my ass, more like five hundred years of dormice. If you touch a hot crack pipe to this place, it'll go up like a Molotov cocktail, so best behavior," Stephen told me in the presence of the real-estate broker, who blinked but said nothing.

The curved, crooked spaces were outlined with huge beams and armed with hyper-efficient Bauhaus cabinetry. The windows thrust out at odd angles into the street. It was like the captain's quarters on a galleon. When the broker advised him to keep the vinyl in the cellar, Stephen smiled condescendingly, but on the other hand he was careful to line his records up along a bearing wall that had floor beams perpendicular.

A short time after we moved downtown, I ran into Elvis on the street. I had been gallivanting about doing nothing much, trying on silk dresses I could have shoplifted in a lipstick case and realizing that even for free they would highlight every drop of sweat like an airport body scan.

We stepped into a café so he could explain his recent doings in his habitual meticulous detail. "I live in Geneva now," he said. "My baby is there. She is so much nice."

"I understand," I said.

"My life is like this. Things pass, and I do with. Whatever and whatever and whatever. Always something. First I am desolated with this pregnancy. And so I see a psychotherapist. We are doing—now—so much beautiful things together. First she take me to Venice, five days. We go also to Tokyo! I am visit her now, but she has a client, and I go walking. So nice surprise to meet you!"

I frowned. "Can't she lose her license?"

"Who will tell them?" he asked. He seemed offended. "Always you think of the state. Always you think they are watching over you. You were born into capitalism! But I was born into chaos. Ah, Tiffany, you fail me. I close my eyes and always I am fucking you. When I see you, I cannot stop thinking this. Let me fuck you now? Why not? No one sees us. Not even you and me. We close our eyes. It stays a secret."

He slipped his hand between my knees and for a second I believed him. I felt we could have done it right there on the barstool and nobody would have known.

I leaned forward and said, "This is exactly, precisely the *mauvaise foi* scene in *L'être et le néant*."

It had never occurred to me before that people actually maybe do have sex they don't want to have. I had always assumed those people had nothing holding them back but inhibitions. But I felt no inhibitions whatsoever. Instead I perceived a powerful longing in my innermost or outermost being (there was no difference, since I generally based appraisals of my affections on the momentary condition of my genitalia) to thaw, spread, and embody the essence of fecundity like a river in springtime.

Yet I also felt strongly that the time might have come to raise myself above the worms by a display of will. I worried that my lust was inhibiting my self-respect and not the other way around. (I was thinking of worms like Omar's wife—she had put the fear of God into me.) In a world of intentional ethics, I was already squirming in a hotel bed with Elvis without a thought in my head. The potential consequences were nil. The risk was hypothetical: If Stephen had been God, able to see around corners, he would have wished to punish my sins. But if Stephen were God, I would have been walking on the other side of the street and Elvis would have made it back to his therapist's office and fucked her instead . . .

The psychotherapist clinched it. "No, thanks," I said as Elvis continued to caress my thighs and arms with great tenderness. "Not today and probably not ever again. Forget it. It's not happening!"

He insinuated his hips between my legs, sighing poetically as his lips approached mine.

"Stop!" I said. I picked up my coffee cup. A mistake.

When the owner of the bar came out from behind the counter, I assumed she meant to come to my aid. But apparently she thought the two of us were bringing down the neighborhood. She asked us to leave. I tried to pay and she grimaced in disgust, waving me out the door with my wallet in my hand.

Elvis was waiting at the next corner. I wailed uncharacteristically in despair and frustration.

"You have showered coffee on me," he said blankly, tilting his head like a shy child. "I am sorry," he added, "but I need a clean shirt for today, please darling! It's so much important."

I gave him a hundred Franken and he sauntered away. I saw him duck from the bustle of the colonnade into a men's clothing store—I couldn't believe it myself—and I turned and ran.

I think approximately seven hundred passersby, including ninety of Stephen's coworkers, saw the handoff of cash and were confirmed in their belief that I was turning tricks to support an ungrateful pimp. But my estimate could be off by a factor of infinity.

*

The apartment was very close to Mancuso's Loft.

Rave music was never my thing. Girls dipping their knees, boys pumping their fists. Too fast to dance to. I had seen Elvis waft across the floor like an air-hockey puck, and I assumed his Latin moves were the only way out. Stephen enlightened me as we stood at the bar sipping ginger ale through straws. "That girl with the head wrap," he said. "Dancehall mouse."

I looked over at a pretty girl with blonde dreadlocks done up in a carpet. Her body was obscured by a loose, longish dress over pants, as if she were doing her western best to conform with the dress code of Yemen. The beat was pushing one-forty, but her hips were circling *extremely* slowly.

The contrast between her movements and the music was startling. She wasn't dancing to it. The soundtrack was a commentary that served to heighten and illustrate her butt.

"Is she hot?" I asked Stephen.

"Nah," he said. "She looks mangy. I'd say she's a tourist, conserving energy because she wants to keep going until Sunday."

"She doesn't want to pick you up? She looks to me like she's disdaining the hoi polloi because she wants to take home the DJ."

"Nobody who goes to clubs ever has sex. They don't have the time."

"Don't they trade sex for drugs?"

"With who? These snuggle-bunnies?" He gestured with his head at the other men at the bar.

"Maybe if the guys had the contraption?"

"Who told you about the contraption?"

"Omar's wife."

"Trust me, they're better off without it. Unless you want this place turning into a lake of body fluids like a dubstep party. It's totally fucking disgusting. I think it's going to change. I hope so. For now I'm taking it on faith that one of these days dubstep will rise above."

"You're so tidy and fastidious."

"I'm attracted to control."

"That's an odd reason to hang out in discos."

"I didn't meet you in a disco."

"Is this a virgin-whore thing?"

"I'm not talking about your songbird sexual mores. I mean your control over your body, the way you eat and dress and get your hair to lie down. You blow me away. It's like you could spend all day at a pig roast eating chocolate ice cream, and then go caving, and come out looking ready to hit the Norfolk Yacht and Country Club."

"It's because I take time to preen," I said. Which is true. My sleekness, when I put my mind to it, resembled that of the arctic loon. But we were both shiny bright as if we had just come out of the autoclave. Immaculate and smooth—as though clinically sterile—unlike his icon of sexlessness Miss Mangy Dread, who was now doing the lambada with a guy whose ad agency was on our street. (I wouldn't have known this, but Stephen knew everybody in the club.) Probably she was his new intern. And I suppose Stephen's look could be better described as fluffy, like a dabchick, which was going to make it hard for him to advance in his career in the cutthroat world of pharmaceutical devices, at least until his temples started to go gray, like a dabchick's.

Stephen put his arm around my shoulder.

"Are we in on the contraption?" I asked.

"I have options that vest in four years."

On weekends I was always home by one o'clock. Stephen would stay out until whenever and then sleep, sleep, sleep. He took a break from birding. I didn't mind. There's something nice about keeping quiet so as not to wake a fluffy man dozing in a fluffy bed. I read fewer novels and more bird books, learning something new every day. Always simple stuff that afterwards I was ashamed to admit I hadn't known.

Like birds nesting on the ground. How was I to know they're so dumb they would build a nest on the ground under a tree, instead of up *in* the tree? So that when the foxes come, the baby birds are doomed. It gave the concept of the Easter egg hunt a sinister new meaning. Hungry little kids out wandering around after a long winter indoors, scanning the ground.

I learned that power lines fry birds. Poof! They're gone. Every time I saw an electric fence on a walk, I imagined little birds sitting on it and poofing into nothingness. That was before Stephen advised me to hold on to an electric fence for a while. It tingles once a second. It might kill a spider, assuming the spider was grounded. I was hard put to imagine why it would slow down a cow.

I learned that kinglets are the smallest birds in central Europe, with eggs no larger than a pea.

Once Stephen was awake, it became hard to concentrate. He had exploited the occasion of our move to hook up his monitors. Sometimes his music sounded like a container ship that had grounded on a shoal and was slowly falling over. Sometimes it sounded like a war movie equalized for projection on the moon. Notions of volume in the post-reggae world put grindcore to shame. Loose sheets of paper on his desk would rise and fall with the bass. If the house had been newer, the roof tiles would have rattled. But it was soft, with fungi and moss as integral elements in the construction, so nothing really rattled much except the glass aftershave bottles on the ceramic shelf over the sink.

We didn't take a birding vacation that year. Without asking me, Stephen rented an apartment in Berlin for the month of June. He wanted to get serious about his music.

We took the slow train, a boxy Swiss IC where you could sprawl out and eat muffins. The German high-speed trains are cylindrical, like airplane fuselages, and you can't open the windows.

In Berne you could always tell yourself, I will lift up mine eyes unto the hills, from whence cometh my help. Berlin was huge and flat, repetitive to the point of bleakness. People were too rich or too poor, and there was nothing to buy. Tawdry crap for teenagers from the sticks, flagship stores, boutiques for Russians, espresso, and fast food. Families shivering in the dark shade of beer gardens, letting their kids run around to warm up.

I rode a heavy bicycle from our rental to the old Tempelhof airport almost every day to see the skylarks fight off the crows with their weapon of song. The crows walked spread out in teams like policemen looking for a corpse in the woods, turning their heads from side to side, staring at the grass with one monocled eye and then the other, but I never saw one eat a baby skylark. Or maybe I always lowered my binoculars in time.

There were lakes with swimmers, boaters, mallards, and coots. Out of town the lakes had grebes and divers, supposedly, but we never got around to leaving town. Stephen slept in. He almost never went to bed before noon. He was occasionally awake early enough to get down to Hard Wax and hear some new dubplate before it closed.

Exactly once, he convinced me to meet him at the Berghain at six o'clock on a Sunday morning. I didn't get in. He had told me to dress for dancing, and I had sneakers on. The other girls in line (I was amazed that there was a line) were bouncing on their toes to keep from teetering on their heels, wearing dresses that would have showed the sweat if they hadn't been so dehydrated their eyes looked like chalk. I hugged myself in my hoodie and shivered, obediently going home on request.

No one was sleek or fluffy in Berlin, not even me. In four weeks I didn't see a single good-looking person on the street. Once in an upscale beer garden in a park I saw young moms and dads who seemed to have gotten some sleep. But everyone else was ashen, and too warmly dressed. It would be in the sixties, and the girls would be wearing army surplus overcoats and ski caps with pompoms, skin all wintry and sallow as if they had consumed nothing but nicotine and pasta for the last six months and lived in dungeons. The boys appeared even on chilly days in T-shirts, their faces flushed with beer. People routinely wore clothes that didn't fit at all, with wrists and belly buttons hanging out.

Except for the space-needle-type TV towers, there was no place to look down at anything. You were always looking out and up until your gaze was arrested by the next moving car.

Every time we ate out we became mildly physically ill.

Accordingly, Stephen insisted we move there. He said Berlin was where he'd always wanted to live. Berne had just been a way of getting to Europe. He had met more interesting people in four weeks in Berlin than in three years in Berne.

Given that so far as I knew he liked nothing better than electronic dance music and shore birds, I had to believe him.

He said the company had a device in development in Berlin, a little pump that had potential as an artificial pancreas, spleen, gallbladder, pituitary gland or anything else you care to name. He said my visa wouldn't let me stay in Switzerland without him unless I got a job all my own, which I would have to apply for from outside the country. Stephen held the keys to my heart.

But wanting to move to Berlin and actually being transferred there are two different things, even for an executive, and Stephen was a researcher.

At home in Berne, I went out to shop for food (a fun thing to do, because you can stroll down the arcades buying one vegetable from each stand) one evening and saw Stephen in a café, poring over papers, sitting next to a strikingly pretty girl with blonde ringlets. I started over, but when I saw she had tousled her hair with mousse to cover bald patches, I backed up and kept on down the arcade trying to find truly fresh radicchio, which is never easy. She looked like a cancer patient, maybe someone Stephen met at a clinical test of the pump, which ought to work for chemo—I had it all mapped out.

When Stephen got home I asked who she was, and he said, "Miss Mangy Dread." That night at the club he had told her she looked like the alien in *Alien*, and the next time he passed the ad agency, the carpet was gone. He went inside to say hello. Her roots had suffered a bit, but she was confident her hair would grow back.

The most conspicuous thing in the shop, he said, was a poster: *Wasserkraft Nein Danke*. Hydroelectric power, no thanks. It was based on the perennial anti-nuclear campaign. But hydroelectric? And there Miss Mangy Dread, whose name was Birke, explained to him that the upper Rhine, since the 1950s, had been "massacred" with a canal and ten "dam steps" all the way from Basel to Iffezheim. The fertile floodplains, gone! High water into the cities of the Ruhr! Basins for holding back the water, but no wet meadows, no frogs, no storks, no life, and why? Because the power companies are taking a license to print money, earning themselves silly on this river! All the consequences carries the public, the taxpayer: flood protection for the cities, because now there are floods, since they build the dams. The loss of biodiversity, of the landscape, of the beauty of the countryside. It is no more a river, only a chain of lakes, and all emitting methane in tremendous quantities! Carbon dioxide is nothing, who cares about carbon dioxide? Methane is seventy, a hundred times worst! And the companies pay the turbines and the dam, nothing else! And they want to build five more steps, from Iffezheim to Mannheim! And all these dams together, they make only so much electricity like one modern gas electric plant!

Stephen resolved at that moment to become an environmental activist. Which of course had to involve getting information from Birke.

Stephen opined that *Wasserkraft Nein Danke* was mostly a way to draw attention to the ad agency. "Her boss is a marketer's marketer. He's good. He showed me a project they did where they got tattoo artists to offer this laundry detergent logo and thousands of people got the tattoo."

"That's pitiful," I said.

"It's out there," Stephen said, "but I have to admit this selling stuff that doesn't sell itself is interesting to me. With a medical device, all you need is an indication and some terminally ill hostages to lay back and let the money wash over you. Selling the idea that the Rhine should be looking like the Yukon is an actual challenge."

"It's man's work," I said. "It's like you're growing up and want to get a real job."

"It's not just the Rhine. There are all these stupid community initiatives advocating energy independence, wanting to put in little hydro plants. It's not like you could even run a milk bottling plant off one of these things, but they chop up the streams into lakes with no way of getting from one to the other. The fish can't get upstream or down. Did you know most fish ladders are dysfunctional, and a huge number of fish die in turbines?"

I was starting to sense that Stephen found me uninteresting relative to Birke.

"I thought fish ladders work," I said. "I mean, I saw one on the Columbia where people were lining up three deep to watch these huge salmon and steelhead leaping up the stairs." I spread my arms to express the immensity of the salmon and trout I had seen.

"That's it," Stephen said. "You see anything smaller? You see any worms going up the fish ladder? Or even a young fish? Fish go where the current is strongest. Most of them don't find the ladders, and on their way back down, they get mangled."

"I see," I said.

"I'm not sure you do," he said. "People regard these bodies of water as rivers because they're damp underfoot, but they have nothing to do with rivers!"

"All right!" I said. "I get the point!"

Birke was printing up posters one at a time on the agency's gigantic photo printer, not sure what to do with them.

Stephen had definite notions. Trumpeting the message of defiance from bus shelters on main roads in every town along the Rhine from Basel to Rotterdam—that's where the posters belonged. It would just take a little money, money that he and Birke would be happy to raise for her boss's new charitable foundation, Global Rivers Alliance.

His first stop would be the bird-related organizations where he was a member. "They're all loaded federal retirees," he explained, "and it's not like they need new optics every year."

"But they're geeks, and Birke's campaign is with-it and happening."

"That's not true," he said. "The campaign is styled to look cool, but de facto the only people willing to espouse unpopular positions are geeks. It's stealth geekdom."

I recalled that Stephen's first appraisal of Birke had included the word mange.

*

Birke taught me to use the gigantic printer. It was slow, so it was fortunate they had a volunteer with a lot of time on her hands.

She told me about the Isar in Munich. It had been a straight, narrow nineteenth-century shipping channel until birders got together and secretly pushed through a very unpopular plan to dismantle the smooth green banks and let the river snake around at random. The stakeholders all hated the idea, mostly because you can't hold a stake in something you've never seen. Then the river was restored, and everybody in the city went down to it and spread out a towel on a broad gravel bank and lay down in the sunshine. In the winter the birds fed and rested, and the fish romped and frolicked, and everybody loved the Isar now and had already forgotten that it was ever a ditch. Someday, she said, people will forget that the Rhine was ever a ditch, just as they will one day lose their selfish enthusiasm for the gravel banks of the Isar and leave them to the plovers.

I immediately saw the overlap between Stephen's theory of geek supremacy and her anti-democratic, anti-participatory elitism.

And the arc linking them both to club music, the collective solitary trance.

Stephen's plan of hitting up birdwatchers for money hit a snag. The bird geeks were pissed off at him. He hadn't given them notice before he ditched the waterbird census, and he appeared to be implicated in the unfavorable outcome of their research into wallcreeper vagrancy. They insisted that the Aare—their river, the Rhine's largest tributary, with its own share of bulkheads and methane bombs—ought to be a higher priority, since the Rhine was, qua river, a collective delusion.

Plus Stephen's aesthetics were not persuasive to them at all one bit. He repeatedly asked Birke to design campaigns around slogans he had come up with, things like "Hydropower: Satan Meets Moloch Uptown" or "Fucked Without a Kiss" (in his view an utterly apt description of the Rhine), reaping nothing but the sidelong look post-punks are always getting from Young People 2.0 that means, "You are *so* unprofessional."

The movement was bankrolled by Birke's boss, George, a princeling with a mane of wavy hair. To his mind, the electronics, chemicals, and paper he needed for his work were ethereal substances as abstract as the gas in his car. Just another form of energy. He was deeply committed, emotionally, to solar power and hydrogen fuel cells. He didn't like wind power. Too oafish. Big masts and turbines plunked down in the landscape, whistling. Under his regime, the planet would lower its top and fly through space, converting sunlight into energy through the medium of the creativity of its passengers, who would all be his friends.

He hit on me, but I ignored him. He would stand behind me and guide my little hands with his big hands as I tugged huge sheets of paperboard out of the machine, whispering into my ear that I worked beautifully. Birke said he had been washed in all the waters, a German expression meaning he had been around the block as well as there and back. Stephen said he was related to a famous and aristocratic publishing family, but Birke said that was his marketing backstory and he came from a sawmill town in the Bavarian Forest and was older than he looked.

I paid little or no attention to George. Still, he took me swimming once. He put our clothes in one of those buoyant watertight knapsacks the Bernese have, and pushed me into the Aare at a campground miles upstream. The river whisked us to the free public pool complex in Marzili. George saw me bearing right and hauled me out by force. There's a dam with a power station downtown, and people who miss the stairway in Marzili die.

Again, I cannot explain why being clasped in his arms and swum across the powerful river did not turn me on, except that it was George. He was not unknowable. No mysteries. Not even a lie. He was bubbly. He shopped for superficial new experiences and shared them. He lacked an event horizon.

Stephen and Birke were always running off to international conferences together. They never claimed they missed me. But when it came time for the BUND Nature Protection Days in Lenzen, they specifically asked me to go along.

I think the idea was that they could work more effec-
tively if Birke appeared to be single, or if Stephen
appeared to be married, or something.

The BUND facilities in Lenzen differ from your typical
convention center. They're basically a room in a hotel,
near the Elbe but not on it, halfway between Berlin and
Hamburg, and hard to get to from either.

The benefits that might accrue to Stephen and Birke
from going to Lenzen were obvious. BUND has half a
million members. Maybe forty of them go to Lenzen.
There's an annual event of the same name in Radolfzell
on the Swiss border in January that draws twelve
hundred. So if you want to make a splash with the BUND
movers and shakers, you'd be better off in Lenzen in
September, where they make up a quarter of the
attendees.

At first I couldn't figure out how Global Rivers Alliance
got invited. But Stephen assured me that just about
anybody can give a talk if he's willing to (important) go
to Lenzen.

And Global Rivers Alliance had been a player from the
word go. Ordinary organizations in the German-speaking
world have names that tout their modest ambitions:
Society for the Preservation of Natural Treasures in
Strunz, Strunz Committee on Woodland Bats, Citizens'
Initiative for the Strunz Wilderness Playground. Not

even "Friends of the Strunz Wilderness Playground," so that you might be tempted to think you could donate ten euros without being enlisted to run a day camp.

Global Rivers Alliance was different. It was modeled on Greenpeace and the WWF. You could donate without ever being asked to do anything but donate.

Prince Kropotkin based his entire theory of anarchism on the German habit of founding and running collectives with strictly limited aims, so we should all be grateful to the twenty-seven competing organizations in Strunz, yet somehow instead they were grateful to organizations like Global Rivers Alliance for lending them a higher purpose.

Birke had reserved a room for Stephen and me in Lenzen castle where the meeting hall was. She took a cheap room in the gun club at the other end of town. Stephen came back to the hotel for breakfast, to keep up appearances, or maybe because at the gun club he wasn't entitled to breakfast. I don't know. The whole weekend, we didn't talk much.

I decided to rent a bike instead of attending the opening session, because someone at breakfast expressed surprise that I had no bicycle. On the Elbe, everybody has a bicycle. I was doing my best to fit in and be inconspicuous, so I decided to rent one on the spot.

The hotel reception told me the shop was right around the corner. I walked the streets of picturesque downtown

Lenzen for twenty minutes reading signs, but I never did find the street where the bike shop was supposed to be. In the end I stopped into a hunting and fishing supply next door to the castle to ask.

Everyone there was familiar with the bike shop. One guy said it was on his way and he would give me a ride. He had a nice convertible. He pulled away from the curb, chatting amiably about birds. He knew what attracted women to Lenzen. Out in the open, the trees by the road flashed down on us in a pattern of golden light and green shade. The enormous meadows stretched to distant solitary oaks. After several miles he pulled over into a large gas station, the size of a small truck stop, behind which was an enormous bike shop like something in an American suburb.

No, not that big. More the size of a 7–11. Berne will skew your sense of scale. The man behind the counter said it was his mother who rented. We drove back into town, landing three doors down from the hunting and fishing supply in an old livery stable with an elderly woman who looked like she'd never been on a bicycle in her life and a few broken-down one-speeds with coaster brakes.

It made sense. Why would locals know where to rent a bad bike? They only knew where to buy a good one.

Renting a bicycle burned up nearly two hours. By the time I stairmastered my creaky bike up to the castle door, I had missed everything worth seeing. The BUND chairman had given a rousing speech, I was told, and the subsequent presentation on the fine points of Natura

2000 financing had been a nimble tour de force of under-statement. But now it was lunchtime.

I ordered something that sounded like grilled fish and turned out to be unimaginably gruesome (lukewarm pickled herring), let it lie, and walked around back to the terrace overlooking the gardens, where there was a frog calling from every tree and a redstart hopping around the fountain. This sucks out loud, I thought.

A harmless-looking man followed me to the porch. He stood next to me, asking me what excursion I was going on that afternoon.

I said, "*Grünes Band*," the green ribbon—the DMZ where the wall used to be. He said it was a good choice and very interesting. We had a pleasant little conversation in passable English.

Now, this guy was not what you'd call hot. But he was polite, and relative to the constant strain of life with Stephen and Birke, it felt like love-bombing from a cult recruiter. I instantly got a huge crush on him. I didn't even care what he looked like. I wanted him to hold me in his arms, pat me on the head, and say, "There, there."

He said his name was Olaf. He reminded me not to miss the excursion to see cranes in the evening. I said I would try to make it.

*

I made the excursion to see cranes.

From the boondocks to the wilderness was a ten-minute bus ride. Someone had gotten to the observation tower before us, an old man with a telephoto lens like a howitzer. He glared at us for touching the balustrade. Instead of climbing up, the group continued down a dry, sandy road through woods and emerged into a clearing behind a windbreak.

The harmless man stood beside me as the sun went down, but the situation was not conducive to romance. There were thirty other people there, shifting their feet in the tedium of waiting for cranes, asking each other to keep their kids quiet or move away from the trees or please put on dark jackets over their white shirts. We stared distractedly at the darkening fen, slapping at mosquitoes that bit us right through our clothes. An unknown woman joined the two of us and began talking about a controversial infrastructure project, encouraged by the harmless man's civility.

At last I heard the cranes. They announced themselves loudly, like geese, but with gurgling trills at the end and no melancholy. First eleven of them—for so long that there was a general consensus that no more would come that night; the guide packed up his scope, and people started back up the road—and suddenly hundreds. They dropped from the sky in dollops, braked, and vanished into the faraway reeds. The woman kept talking to the harmless man about rail-versus-road. I walked to the edge of the marsh and raised my binoculars.

If I hadn't known what they looked like from books, I would never have guessed from seeing them at that distance. They were sock puppets with red heels poking over the reeds a mile away, dull gray in the dusk.

After the cranes had landed, the geese passed overhead in so many Vs that they merged into Xs and covered the entire sky like a fishnet stocking. My eyes turned damp. The harmless man smiled tenderly.

We returned by bus to the hotel, where I found Stephen and Birke in the lounge. They were chatting with a couple of new media types from Berlin who had designed a campaign to increase public acceptance of wild bees. The bees on their marketing materials were fuzzy, happy spheres—no thorax, no abdomen, no stinger, just a friendly ping-pong ball with tiger stripes. The people of Berlin had welcomed this animal with open arms.

Stephen and Birke wanted to get in on the secret of big government grants. They acted like gossip columnists sucking up to movie stars.

I drifted to the bar and listened to a long, one-sided discussion of tree frog courtship led by an aging softy in a clerical collar. Slain by half a glass of wine, I struggled upstairs to bed.

I woke at six, alone, and went downstairs to my bicycle, intending to ride out to the river. I wanted to see where the levee had been moved away from the river to make room for birds. It had been one of the excursions the day before, when I was taking in the glories of life in the DMZ. It felt unjust to have missed it, since it had an explicit Global Rivers theme.

It was pitch dark and foggy. I don't know why that surprised me. The year had gotten away from me. Indian summer had fooled me into thinking six o'clock was already time to grab my boots and binoculars and run out before it was too late.

Stubbornly, it stayed dark. Whenever the bike stopped moving, the dynamo stopped turning and the light vanished, leaving me blinded from its former glare on the fog. I stood at the spot where the dike had been relocated (the sign by the road allowed no doubts) and saw that everything around me was black. Everything. But I could hear birds: geese grumbling and complaining like couples fighting over blankets, lapwings elbowing each other, a curlew begging God for blessed sleep. Something big passed over my head in near silence, just a whoosh of feathers. There were no songbirds, just the crypto-human voices of avian insomniacs, and I started to sob uncontrollably.

For the first time in years—or perhaps since infancy, when I hadn't known other people existed—I was certain I was alone, and my prompt gut reaction was to abandon all hope.

Now, in town, you never know whether the neighbors are home. Even in the backcountry of Yosemite, there are those other people with a pass. Nearly anywhere you go, someone might hear or see you. But not on a levee by the Elbe two miles from the nearest town in dense fog at six o'clock on a Sunday morning in September. They say in space no one can hear you scream, but why would a person with a sense of dignity scream anywhere else?

Much later, reading a map, I noticed that the ninety-degree bend in the river—the reason they had moved the dike—had an old traditional name: "The Evil Place."

Fifth wheels always cry! one might protest. But at the time, Stephen's affair with Birke seemed perfectly fair to me. I hadn't forgotten about Elvis. My relationship with Stephen was contractual. By coming along to Lenzen, I had signed on the wrong dotted line. It was my responsibility to face the consequences.

The first rays of the sun brought hope, if only that I might soon see something.

The second set of rays, after a brief glimpse of something horizon-like, lit the fog from behind, and the abyss-slash-void became a gray wall. I rode back to a place where there had been less fog, an island of semi-transparent air where it was warmer, and sat down next to the bicycle, waiting for the first trees to appear. They appeared. But sunrise was still a long way away. I gave up and rode back.

At breakfast Stephen wanted to know where I had spent the night.

"Don't you remember?" I said. "We talked in the bar to those communication designers and then I went to bed? You are so on drugs."

*

Birke's talk was a triumph. The time was ripe for *Wasserkraft Nein Danke*. She could be as grandiose and radical as the day is long. She was not accountable. The privilege of youth. Men three times her age swore to borrow her idea and take the lead in implementing it. They had waited too long to make the dangers of hydro-electric power clear. Young people (why exactly twenty-somethings are considered so vital to protest movements, I never figured out, seeing as how they never vote and have no money) would follow the call, power companies would bend the knee, Birke would get free banner ads on everybody's website.

Stephen and Birke held court at their information table, handing out exquisite pamphlets on visibly recy-cled paper (not the white kind), framed by the apocalyp-tic blue of a very large *Wasserkraft Nein Danke* poster. Behind them, water plunged from a spillway. That's all the poster showed: water in a state of collapse—the real, existing state of collapse that every dam represents, the collapse of a river and its ecosystem. And posing in front of it, Stephen and Birke, ready to be swept away.

As I stood there drinking apple juice from the buffet and watching them, Olaf touched my arm.

We sat next to each other on the back porch and looked out and down at the walled gardens. He told me how much he enjoyed visiting the green ribbon, where nothing much had ever been built. He loved the stillness, the emptiness. It was something worth fighting for.

I had seen the emptiness, and I wasn't sure I liked it. Or maybe it wasn't all that empty where he was. I asked him whether he had children.

He claimed partial responsibility for a herd of rare sheep and explained that you need sheep to maintain the emptiness.

"What about the stillness?" I asked. "Don't they wear bells and bleat?"

He admitted that even birds, tempting as it may be to stylize their presence as stillness, are actually pretty loud.

We walked down into the lower garden and sat on a bench. He looked into the pond and remarked favorably on the lack of goldfish. I thought of all the spawn-guzzling carp I had admired in the past and felt abashed. I shrank at the vulgarity of raptures over beauty, nature's most irrelevant and unnecessary quality.

That is, I couldn't quite approve of the way the harmless man looked, but I was ready to follow him around like a puppy. He was that reassuring.

I stood up to escape back into the hotel. He remained seated. As we shook hands I couldn't help noticing how close his wedding ring (Germans wear them on their right hands) was to what Allen Ginsberg called the center of the flesh, and I realized I had a problem.

After Global Rivers Alliance's successful Nature Protection Days, Birke proceeded to Berlin. She vanished into her accustomed social milieu, whatever that was. Her internship in the environmental movement was about to end, and Berlin was where she was in school, studying media design. She had to visit old friends and see about a sublet.

Stephen and I returned to Berne without her. He looked spent and weary.

When Birke reappeared in Berne to pack her things, he cheered up, but her going-away party may have included some kind of unpleasant scene. Perhaps their parting.

A week later, he went to visit her and cheered up again for several minutes. I mean the minutes between when his taxi arrived from the airport early Monday morning and when the alarm went off so he could go to work. He was down.

The posters went up in three languages in bus shelters all the way to Rotterdam. Birke gave interviews to curious reporters. A magazine devoted to social entrepreneurship and social investment labeled her one to watch.

"Social entrepreneur" meant something different in old books than it does now. The new definition didn't fit Birke. There was nothing capitalistic about Global Rivers Alliance. The impact investment community would sponsor a project if you promised them thirty percent, and pat themselves on the back for not actually drinking your blood. They couldn't get their head around rivers.

But they liked Birke. She gave great interviews, effervescing with ideas. In person she was pretty enough to surprise people who had only seen the publicity photos. She became known.

Stephen didn't become known. He was the pale figure with pale hair in the background, barely distinguishable from the wall.

Stephen and I had about twenty fights, all including the following exchanges:

"You're going to work for your *girlfriend*."

"No, she's working for me. I'm the executive director."

"*Geschäftsführer* is an administrative post. She calls the shots, and it's George's money."

"I'm the one investing. My labor is worth more than George's money." (I had to hand it to him for that one.)

"You're throwing away your life to move to a town with *dubstep* [tone of contempt]."

Baleful glare, followed by allusions to migratory waterfowl.

"Why not wait for your transfer to come through?"

"How long do you think I've been waiting already?"

Our fights had a strange new quality: earnestness. Regular contact with the environmental movement had turned Stephen into a man who spoke his mind clearly and purposefully.

Before Stephen turned earnest, we never had fights.

Berne, my beloved Berne, was looking to the earnest Stephen more and more like a cobblestone prison yard. He began saying the stent was antiquated and that his

coworkers were intellectual midgets now that all the
good people had been transferred to Topeka or Berlin.
And all the while the Rhine climbed higher, rolling and
writhing in its corset of stone, moaning to be free. Ships
bobbed through its lifeless locks, electric power flowed
from its bloodstained turbines, the river had been dead
for eighty years and there wasn't a goddamn thing anyone
could do about it, except work day and night and see
Birke on weekends. She was more than willing to marry
him. Her political persuasions admitted of no other
stance. "No human being is illegal!" she would insist, as
though she had picked up Stephen in a camp in Chad. She
thought marriage would solve all their problems. He
could live with her, collect welfare, and save the world.

The fights went on until he got a scholarship to study
chemistry. George could supposedly only afford to pay
him six hundred euros a month. That's plenty to retire on
in Berlin, Birke had assured him, but it's illegal to be that
poor unless you're a German or married to one. Stephen
had staged fights with me to ease the pain of deep-sixing
his career. After the letter from the Technical University
arrived, he remarked that taking a few years off to get a
master's would be a gap on his résumé, but not nearly as
bad as working for Global Rivers Alliance.

Birke had no chance against me. By staying at home—as
I had done from the beginning (I seldom slept with Elvis
anywhere else!)—I had made plain to Stephen that I was
the type who stays at home, come what may. Better,

worse, sickness, health, all the various combinations that can go either way depending on who's pushing harder. If you believe in marriage as an institution the way Stephen did, one thing you definitely don't want is to try it more than once. If Stephen married Birke, the marriage would end, because for her it was one option among many. Whereas if he stuck with me and saw her on weekends, he and I would one day share a headstone. Game, set, and match Tiffany.

But Stephen didn't give notice. He kept holding out for a transfer.

In November, he refused a transfer to Topeka. When I suggested he call Omar and ask what Topeka is like, he laughed. In return for his refusal, the company issued him a C-class Mercedes and a little tiny handheld computer. He had been tested for gumption and not found wanting. Or maybe it was a bribe.

He sold the Volkswagen without telling me. It was weeks before I knew where the Mercedes was parked. I was never allowed to touch the computer.

I was desperately unhappy. I remembered the cranes and even the fog on the levee as though remembering the land of lost content. The Housman heaven: I see it shining plain, the happy one-way highways. And the Bialik heaven (as per T. Carmi): the distant islands, the lofty worlds we saw in dreams that evict us to dwell under the open sky (as absolute vagrants, seeking always those sunny days with a light fresh wind) and make our lives a hell.

Stephen looked haggard. Mentally, he was unrecogniz- able. "Birds are quantum," he would say blandly. "If you can even figure out where they're hiding, it's too late to see them as they truly are. There's no such thing as bird-watching. It's an illusion for stupid people."

During the week, he worked full time and then some. He had to clock as many hours as colleagues who spent Saturday afternoons at the lab, all while running Global Rivers Alliance in his spare time. Most nights he went straight to bed before eleven and thrashed around while he slept. On weekends he flew to Berlin. The round-trip by train would have eaten up twenty hours. My pin money was going down, down, down.

On weekends I was alone. I tried snowshoeing. It was too loud, too raucous, too much hilarity, too much money, plus Stephen said I might accidentally squish grouse. The Bat Society (I tried them next) was on winter hiatus, its bats snoozing away in cellars and caves. The women in hand-knit mohair sweaters and silk scarves assured me that bats are soft and clean with wings like kid gloves and that I need not fear them. The astronomy club seemed more promising. I spent an evening standing next to a goon huffing steam in the cold and saw the red spot on Jupiter, which looked just like on TV.

My misery was firm and unshakable. The old city of Berne was my natural habitat. It was where I felt at home, where I wanted to be. I didn't want to leave. Berne was where I could become most completely myself—posses-sive, shrewish, lonely. There was nothing to retard my self-actualization.

*

George's new intern was very good-looking and a fine media designer, but not much to talk to. She knew nothing about environmental issues and cared less.

Consequently, Stephen was physically revolted by her. As if her failure to notice what was going wrong with the planet was linked to a black, spongy degeneration of her brain that might be contagious.

Even my own desire to improve my moral standing repelled him. "What's that got to do with the price of tea in China?" he would snarl. "Breaking up with Elvis is not the same as being a decent person. It's utterly irrelevant to anything and everything. It's a matter of absolute ethical indifference whether you screw around. The world is not a better or worse place because you do or don't screw around."

The poster campaign hadn't cost Stephen any real heartache. But once the money ran out, Global Rivers Alliance's self-promotion migrated online, and to his sorrow, every single person who toyed with the idea of wiring two dollars to George first felt compelled to debate the merits of *Wasserkraft Nein Danke* with him. Most were themselves running tiny organizations that had arisen by spontaneous generation or mitosis. No one had supporters. Stephen spent hours writing closely argued defenses of himself and his aims. Each one unique, because you can't copy anything anymore without getting caught. Rushed, because anyone who didn't get an answer within fourteen hours would write again with more questions.

Eventually he tried one of those services that limit your communication to a hundred and something characters, and it saved him. He began pouring his energy into aperçus and bon mots. That was better. His task now was to strike a jaunty pose from which to launch scathing witticisms about the energy industry. Instead of preaching to the converted, he would sit on the couch with them watching the news and make snide remarks. But they still wanted clever new aphorisms every day.

The Rhine Conference was not open to the public like Nature Protection Days. It was for professionals. Stephen and Birke worked hard every weekend to prepare. Sworn to present their work to an audience of experts, they had to figure out what it was. They had goals, partners, approaches, and a campaign—all the things you can have without actually having done anything—but they needed projects. *Wasserkraft Nein Danke* was not a project. It was a negation. The project to end all projects. When he got back, he made it sound as though he'd had five minutes to get ready and been dragged there by his hair. "Never again," he said.

"Who was there?"

"The usual suspects. The BMVBS, the WWF."

I waited for more information and finally said, "Were they not nice to you?"

"They paid no attention to me. It's like they can smell that I know nothing about ecology or hydrology or engineering. Maybe if you're actually legit, you emit this pheromone and they can smell it."

"Maybe you need scientist outfits, like functional microfiber outerwear."

"God, Tiff," he said. "You are so ignorant."

"I was kidding," I said.

"Yeah, right. So at the conference I keep asking these bright, intelligent questions, like I think an inquisitive amateur is what the world needs now. And they answer me with patience and fortitude like I'm a fucking four-year-old. Believe me, my suits are not the problem."

"But you're an activist running a media campaign. They know that."

"I know I'm a self-styled activist promoting a slogan. You don't have to remind me." He looked down at his hands as if checking for dirt.

He was silent for three minutes, as long as the minutes of silence that pepper the conversations in *Women in Love* by D.H. Lawrence, and finally said: "The laws are all in place. The people are sovereign, telling the politicians what to do, which is to maximize economic growth without losing any copyrightable DNA. The politicians are doing their job. So it's the investors you need to lobby, not the bureaucrats who are trying like hell to slow development down. And these are the guys who can sense that my experience is in inflatable stents. They can tell I'm on this delusion-of-grandeur mission to teach and inform them why they haven't saved the rivers yet. To them, I'm the ultimate smartass, like some asshole from McKinsey. They hate me. The only thing they think laymen are good for is to supply emotional arguments that might make somebody put up with nature. But they know it won't work. Because if you have a plant you don't like the looks of on your lawn, or a bug that looks weird, you're going to kill it, unless you're a total sap. So all the nature lovers get this training and these jobs and make out like they're master technicians of the ecosphere, but they're just saps. Because nobody knows how the ecosphere works. It just wants to be left alone. Life is what happens when you leave it alone. It's circular! But nobody wants to leave it alone. They want to love it. Love of nature is a contradiction in terms. It's the thing everybody says nobody has enough of, and it's this totally nonexistent personality trait. The myth of biophilia. Loving living things at your own expense, being happy that they're out there somewhere, living their lives, where you never see them. Give me a break. What a fucking joke."

"Like in the 'Rime of the Ancient Mariner,'" I said.

"What's that got to do with anything? You never listen to me."

"I mean about loving living things. It's like when he says, O happy living things no tongue, their beauty might declare, and the albatross falls off his neck into the sea."

"Albatross on his neck? Why doesn't it fly away?"

"It's dead. He shot it with a crossbow. That's why the ship was under a curse. They tied it around his neck."

"How did they tie it on? With the wingtips in front, like a cape?"

"They tied it on a string, I'm pretty sure. I know it's a huge bird, like a turkey, but I mean, this is the British navy. They had punishments like keelhauling and confinement to the bowsprit. The albatross is nothing."

"The albatross was dead."

"But the water snakes were alive! He looks over the side and sees the slimy things that crawl with legs upon the slimy sea, and he realizes there's nothing better in the world, and he says, O happy living things no tongue, their beauty might declare. Because the water snakes were alive, and he was alone on a ship full of dead people."

Stephen paused and said, "The key word is slimy. If they hadn't been slimy, they would have been lunch. I mean it. Disgust is a prerequisite for love."

I was hurt. "Yeah, like you look at birds and think, words cannot express the vertiginous, retching horror."

"I wouldn't put a bird in my mouth."

I remembered the long pointy bill Rudi was constantly cleaning bug bits off and his long toes like spider legs and said, "Me neither."

Stephen added, "If people spent more time being disgusted, the world would be a better place. People might revolt. Like vomit."

I began to speak, but let it pass.

"I give you your space, right?" His voice was tired. "I'm not one of those guys who comes in the bathroom when you're taking a shit. I don't want to know! And with the birds, I'm always giving them their space. I let them do their thing. They might as well be plush toys to me. I don't even know how they breathe. Who cares what they want out of life? Slimy shit to eat, probably. So I'm mind-ing my own business and letting them mind theirs, and everybody's happy. And I'm going around thinking I'm the ultimate bird-lover, but then when I talk to real activists, I feel like this."

He held up his hand as though giving me the finger, but the only finger raised was his pinkie.

"To them," he continued, "every bird is unique, with different needs, incredibly complex, and nature is gone and never coming back. They're just fighting to get more wells in the game park. They want all the animals to have some water rights and maybe live past tomorrow in subsidized housing. They don't give a shit about game-changers like let's bomb the Rhine back into the stone age, because you can't predict what the results will be. They're like, let's use this public policy instrument to expand this puddle over here and attract some waders. And I realize the point of running a media campaign is A, to delude like-minded people into thinking there are other like-minded people and B, to make them think things are way better than they are. Like, people of Europe, decide your future! Make your choice, whether you want to have wild rivers! But there's no democracy and no wild rivers. Whether or not everything gets fucked up beyond all recognition is going to be decided by the same people who decide everything else. Rich companies. And they can't put their money to work without fucking shit up. When they try, like by investing in something nonexistent like credit default swaps instead of something tangible like renewable energy, we rag on them even harder. When the Taliban blew up the giant buddhas, the mistake they made was saying they did it as a matter of principle and not as an investment. Principles are inherently dead. They're based on past experience. If you say you have principles, you've just admitted you have no hope of ever getting rich."

As for Birke, he had gotten as far as Banja Luka, the bar in Kreuzberg where he was supposed to meet her. The weather was cold, but the outside tables were open for smokers. There he saw her with another man, and he became very, very angry. In his rage, he realized he had never really been attracted to Birke. What fascinated him was the vulnerability of European rivers.

I asked who the guy was.

"That guy you're so into. The harmless guy."

"No way," I said.

"Yeah, what a weasel. But you know Birke. Anything for the cause."

People talk a lot about midlife crisis, the momentary stress that arises when you finally slack off. The sublime flash of greenish light as the curtain of the sanctuary rips, when poets start reviewing books and programmers take jobs in quality control.

It has nothing on unrequited love. Stephen stopped sleeping. He spent his nights staring at the TV with the sound off. He took Provigil so he could go to work. He looked weak and ashen as a ghost. On my knees by the couch, I begged him to take a few weeks off.

He quit his job. He abandoned the stent and the stock options as if he had never heard of money.

I tried to take it philosophically. I had enough cute clothes to last ten years, if I washed them carefully in the soft water they have in Berlin.

Global Rivers Alliance would continue to be headquartered in Berne. George, the president, was paying rent to himself—never a bad idea for a small businessman—and Switzerland is a fine address for any charitable foundation, like a cross between Aspen and The Hague. Stephen would operate out of a defunct machine shop on a concrete slab on the east side of Berlin, sharing a table with other freelancers he'd never met. Imagining the marble floors and receptionist of the home office in Berne would help his visitors tolerate the sound of officemates slurping lattes and nattering away on video conference calls.

Stephen the underemployed non-birder was a lonely person.

Secretly he was working to create majestic panoramas of mud where birds could plunge their beaks to just shy of the eyeballs, but all he ever talked about was wind, solar, and the need to invest in a smart power grid. His emotional detachment from his talking points made him strident.

He had been right about one thing. GRA's main line item was his opportunity cost. Birke wanted to reissue the *Wasserkraft Nein Danke* posters tinted red as a cascade of foaming blood. According to Birke, blood was trending with young people (vampires), plus it was time for a knockout punch.

If he had still been working in Berne, he could have printed and distributed the red posters with his pocket money whether George liked them or not. Now they had to sell their ideas, not give them away, and in the creativity glut that was Berlin, not even George was buying.

Our place in Berlin was several hundred yards from party central, meaning roughly speaking the Kottbusser Tor subway station. We lived on the ground floor in the back, with access to the street through a massive wooden gate.

Our windows looked out on a muddy courtyard. The loveless gray coating of cement that had been slapped on the brick wall opposite was corroding to a height of fifty feet. Above that, it had flaked off entirely, leaving the clumsy, gap-filled brickwork disconcertingly bare all the way to the sky. When I leaned my head out the window and looked up, I could see a bit of blue, on nice days.

Outside the gate was a playground where teenagers drank vodka day and night. It opened on to a park that faced a bridge over a canal. The youth of many nations gathered on the bridge to play guitars and drums at all hours. We felt lucky to be in the back, except when the youth of many nations found our gate ajar and slipped inside to take a shit.

Our apartment was both larger and more modern than the one in downtown Berne. But perceptions are relative. Berlin was known for high-ceilinged rentals dating from the turn of the second-to-last century that reflected the tastes of an ascendant middle class. It lacked quaint medieval niches like our place in Berne. We had a third-tier proletarian's apartment, and it felt like the tenement it was. Dim and dank, with uneven walls. I counted forty-four bicycles in the morass below our windows, some tightly bound to the drainpipes with clematis. Under them were plastic toys that would outlast the building next door by millennia.

My budget was a little different than it had been in Berne, but Stephen let me buy paint. For several days he swore to refrain from buying maxi singles, before he remembered that DJing is a way to make money.

In spring the flies returned in force. They were a constant presence all winter. The courtyard had three large garbage cans for bio-trash. The lids were irreparably crooked and the neighbors were—I don't know whether inebriated or simply careless—somehow not in command of their actions, so that the ground around them was strewn with banana peels and melon rinds. When the temperature dropped below freezing, the compost froze solid and couldn't be emptied, and when the temperature rose the maggots swarmed.

I am proud (as a housewife) to say that I don't know whether Rudi ate flies. But the combination of high wall, missing bricks, and bugs made me think he could have made a home with us, had he lived and Berlin been at 15,000 feet.

My German was getting better, and I met people. I learned that I wasn't a feminist. Even men in their seventies, talking to me after meetings about an impending block party or the proper sorting of garbage, would raise their eyebrows when I said I had followed my husband from Philadelphia to Berne and then Berlin. I couldn't come up with a step I'd taken in life for my own sake. On my own behalf, to make myself happy, I'd done all kinds of things, all of them with the aim of staying close to a man. It hadn't occurred to me to be ashamed of myself. I'd thought love was a socially acceptable motivation. But to right-thinking Germans, I was a mindless whore, and historically I had never felt more normal than in the company of other mindless whores (e.g., Elvis).

I met someone who was the right kind of wife. Her husband played trumpet in a ska outfit whose contrabass player sometimes improvised to Stephen's minimal drive-by or whatever it was called that week. When I met her she had a kid on her shoulders and a baby on the ground at her feet, and she was talking gaily about India with a vendor of Indian junk at the flea market. The vendor was impressed, and I, too, was impressed. She was young the way an actual young person is young. Not like weary, defeated Stephen and me. She confirmed my suppositions about her sterling qualities as a wife by inviting me for coffee and serving a cake she had baked herself using yeast. I never did understand yeast.

Like me, she had moved to Berlin to be with her husband. The key difference was the kids. I envied her with a pang. An educated woman with little kids (I didn't imagine her having acquired them by any other means than hot sex) is a model of feminist, as well as feminine, virtue. Even her struggle to get strangers to take the kids off her hands is a feminist cause. Her work, bringing up the model citizens of tomorrow, is something society feels it ought to value and is constantly proposing as potentially eligible for pension benefits, unlike my work, which neither involved actual labor nor was anything but an end in itself, on good days, and otherwise not even that.

The next time we had coffee, she said she had been a Slavic languages major at an international program in Krakow and abandoned her studies when the first baby came. That was about nine months after Hermann's band played Krakow. She had barely remembered him, but she looked him up online. She hadn't planned to drop out, but it was absolutely impossible to be an adequate mother and have a life, she said. She didn't resent her children. She said they were every bit as interesting as verbs.

Olaf, the harmless man, e-mailed the Global Rivers Alliance info-address to invite us to a slide lecture on storks at a NABU meeting in Pankow.

Stephen said, "This might interest you. Everyone else on the planet over the age of twelve has something better to do with their time."

My emotions at the prospect of seeing Olaf could best be described as ecstatic moping.

It was quiet out in Pankow. I could hear chickadees chirping as I stumbled over the cobblestones. When Olaf saw me, he smiled.

I probably projected a sense of relief. I had been half expecting him to arrive with Birke on his arm and her name tattooed on his neck. "It's great to see you!" I said.

"It's great to see you!" he said, turning away to shake someone's hand.

I felt: He knows I have a crush on him, he knows I know about his thing with Birke, he knows it hurts me, and he knows I don't hold it against him. In short, he knows I'm desperate, yet submissive, and that he can do anything he wants with me, especially ignore me. I stood there with a lost look, feeling as though I had been ordered and not picked up, as the Germans say.

His presentation was designed to promote tourism to the European Stork Village of Rühstädt. The Rühstädt storks nest on every available roof. When they return from Africa in March, they eat worms. Then they eat the town's plentiful frogs. They have kind eyes and patient smiles. Not just any town can become a European Stork Village (ESV). There is a strict evaluation process, and if the interests of, say, industrialized agriculture are put above those of storks, the town will be bounced right out of the program and its storks deployed elsewhere. But Rühstädt valued its storks, which are fun for the whole family. The town was like a safari park, with storks climbing all over everything, catching mice, thrashing the life

out of lizards, following cows around. It was like vaca-
tioning in the baboon enclosure at the zoo, except they
had no thumbs and couldn't grab anything out of your
hands and tear it apart. They were after other quarry.
Human beings to storks were just a way of mowing the
lawn, and nothing pleases them more than a whiff of
decaying socialism. If you plot Germany's stork nests on
a map, you can see where East Germany used to be,
because it's where the storks are now. The ESV Rühstädt,
Olaf concluded, offers the ultimate in stork experience.
The audience was free to infer its superiority to state
government-approved SVs and the various other self-
styled/consensus SVs that haunt self-published municipal
media. Immediately after the talk, Olaf approached me
and asked if I would like to go out somewhere for a drink.
He didn't even take time to ditch the local chairman. He
just herded me toward the coat rack. I said yes.

We agreed to try a bar that was a few feet away on the
corner. We looked in the window (skinheads, bikers) and
kept walking.

It was a humid night with warmth in the wind. It was
very dark. Inside of a dozen yards, the darkness and other
factors made the distance back to the meeting room and
the tram stop seem unbridgeable and the distance to
Stephen and Birke intergalactic. We walked for five
minutes, passing two or three more bars. I thought maybe
Olaf was so restless in my presence that he was walking
at random. Instead he touched my arm in front of a run-
down townhouse and said, "This is it." He opened the
door with an old four-sided socialist key and shepherded

me inside. Still in the hallway, standing by the mailboxes, he said, "I've been wanting to do this," and put his arms around my waist.

It was not what I had been expecting. He was sweet, and serious, and his mustache tickled. We crept to his rented room and had sex in a very single-minded way.

He said he was a lobbyist with the European Environmental Bureau and had friends in Pankow. He was a close follower of political developments and the soul of calm, which I suppose is a chicken-egg problem. He called the policies he was trying to influence "my themes," as in my cards, the hand I've been dealt. The things it has been given to me to care about. While Stephen was busy getting all fired up to run hard all day every day as if what activists do is be active, Olaf sat coolly regarding his hand and deciding which cards to keep face down. Where I was concerned, his strategy had apparently been to abstract me from the presence of anyone we both might know and get me into bed before considering consequences and further options. He said with surprise that he had not slept with Birke, although she was a very persuasive speaker and clearly an asset to Global Rivers Alliance.

We didn't talk about anything personal. We had more sex. I don't think I laughed once. Then it got to be about eight o'clock, and we went to sleep.

Stephen was not going to be happy.

*

Stephen was not happy. When I saw him again the next afternoon, he greeted me with a hard-on and the word "homewrecker." I didn't mind. My privates were so raw from overuse that I couldn't think of any other body part. When I closed my eyes I still felt Olaf's dick. But I felt guilty about reducing Olaf to body parts the way he had reduced me, so I kept my eyes open to watch Stephen fuck me, which he did as if his marriage depended on it.

Stephen never had a strategy about anything. He just went ahead and did stuff, then tried retrospectively to figure out why.

It made him a pawn of fate, relative to Olaf. All those contradictions occasioned by his passion to make his dreams come true while recursively extracting unrealistic from realistic dreams in order to denounce the former as vanities. Even his fucking was binary, a sorting process by which certain practices could be tried and found wanting or approved and accorded benchmark status.

What went on inside me was something else. I lay there in an aura worthy of Prince Myshkin, possessed by indeterminacy, feeling Olaf vividly and somehow (keeping our conversation impersonal was presumably part of his strategy) unable to recall that he was a married man who lived hundreds of miles away.

Wasserkraft Nein Danke reached critical mass. Dozens of organizations had jettisoned its banner from their site and adopted the slogan themselves. They stopped waffling on hydro-electric and began solidly advocating decentralized solar and bat-safe wind. Donations to Global Rivers Alliance were down.

And so was public support for the Green Party and environmental causes generally. The electorate fumed that it had been deceived all those years into thinking dams were somehow green. It folded its collective arms and pouted. The mainstream media ridiculed *Wasserkraft Nein Danke* as the single whiniest own goal in league history.

But Birke's idea had succeeded in moving public debate to the left. No one wrote anymore about whether hydro-electric power was good or bad, only about whether it was entirely necessary to remove all the dams on the Rhine at a cost of billions of euros. Commentators on the far right demanded that the existing dams on the Rhine be spared.

Of course, what effect the public discourse might have on actual construction projects was anybody's guess. Such projects lumbered to their feet over periods of decades and moved, or melted, as inexorably as glaciers. Saving the world wasn't exciting or dynamic. It was more like the pharma pipeline, except the malady it hoped to cure had pockets so deep they could have swallowed the environmental movement and every other eccentricity in civil society without a burp. You might stop them building a dam at a given site this decade, but maybe they never wanted to. The pockets—huge, deregulated private utilities—were mutually opaque and nominally in competition, but somehow or other they always seemed to share priorities. Or rather a single priority: freedom. They wanted to be able to plan as if nothing else on Earth existed. Their chief responsibility was to their investors, who wanted them to be the best pockets they could be. Places to store value. Deep and capacious, with space for liquid billions and no holes.

For the moment, industry backed away from the rivers. It started asking for woodlands for wind turbines and fracking as an alternative to lignite coal. Birke had won.

It was nearly impossible for me to see Olaf. When he came to Berlin, he was in meetings all day, and in the evenings he was expected at home. I didn't have money to go lurking around Bonn for a week, waiting for his wife to give him a minute off. Stephen and I were so broke I was buying food at the flea market, fruits and vegetables of no known provenance and noodles that dissolved when the water boiled.

Olaf and I had coffee downtown in absurdly public venues like the Sony Center. He put his dates with me on his expense account as meetings with Global Rivers Alliance, the only way he could account to anyone for the lost time. He tried to schedule another evening talk that would keep him in Berlin overnight, but all the relevant club meetings were booked a year in advance. He told me not to worry my little head about pumped storage hydro-electric, because solar had a habit of delivering energy at peak demand.

I was in love. I thought about him constantly. I was terrified my animal cravings would die down before I got a chance to fuck him again, and all that good horniness would go to waste.

Olaf said his feelings were similar, and having taken months to consider tactics, decided on a dinner date to talk strategy with a locally prominent radical priest in the middle of Saxony-Anhalt. It seemed like an odd choice, but it would (a) keep him away overnight, since his wife could hardly demand he drive home from Saxony-Anhalt, (b) involve a priest, further contributing to her disorientation, and (c) give me a chance to see the Elbe, that meandering canal whose neatly scalloped banks, lined with Wilhelminian hunting lodges, Birke so readily compared to those of the Amazon. The priest would meet us for dinner in Breitenhagen, a village distinguished by its possession of a motel.

We had dinner in the motel bar. Olaf and Gernot, the high-church Anglican pastor of Wittenberg, talked shop. They seemed to know each other well. The conversation was over my head, mostly involving those government agencies I can never keep straight. Even in a single German state (there are sixteen) there will be a ministry of the environment, transportation and reactor safety, known until two years ago by some completely different name, coexisting happily with a department of energy and the environment, an institute for transportation and consumer protection, and a bureau of renewable energy, agriculture and forestry. Olaf paid attention to more than one state at a time, plus the federal government and the counties.

And so did the radical priest. It was somehow part of his work as a fisher of men. He conducted it with regal seriousness while picking daintily at macaroni and cheese.

He was not the person I was expecting to be presented to as somebody's slam piece. I based this assessment on his table manners and the quality of his suit. I felt reduced to my lowest common denominator, as if I hadn't been reduced enough already. So the only thing about their conversation that really stuck in my mind was how often they said the names of other women. They called them "colleagues," and I was jealous. I'd seen enough German lady environmentalists to know that most of them could be my lesbian grandmother, but I felt inferior to them all. They were colleagues, and what was I? They were out there somewhere being taken seriously for doing serious work, saving nature from whatever, while I studiously fucked not only their husbands but even my own as though miming reproductive acts were my sole aim in life. I could be defined as an irrelevant distraction even for Stephen, who was obviously fonder of Birke. I was the expense of spirit in a waste of shame. Unless sex is worth something. I mean, if Marx was right—if sex is work and marriage involves sex—then I was creating value added. Otherwise, I was a distraction. Olaf could have ordered schnitzel or a penniless Ukrainian instead.

That train of thought may have been inspired by his choice of "sausage salad," a salad made almost entirely of bologna and raw onions drizzled with vinegar. He piled it on to slices of bread with a knife and ate it in a way that was hard to watch. I had forgotten all about men with simple tastes. When a guy sets you on a life list with blatantly aspirational qualities, you feel exclusive, but maybe all you did was say yes the way the bottle of Chateau Lafite says yes when he takes it down from the rack. The longer Olaf talked to Gernot, the more challenging and purposeful his work seemed. Maybe he had taken me on for contrast.

The sordidness of my reflections was dragging my mood through the cocoa powder, as the Germans say, and I recalled that the author of *Philosophy in the Boudoir* did not come to a good end, so I joined in the conversation. "I like birds," I said.

"I will never understand the attention paid to birds," Olaf promptly replied. "They are by far the most exhaustively researched vertebrate group. They are conspicuous, diurnal, and enjoy a high level of general acceptance. Far more vulnerable now are the small mammals." He touched my hand (Germans eat with their hands on the table) when he said "small mammals."

"Birds without small mammals would get hungry," Gernot agreed.

I laughed nervously. Sad to say, I inferred at the time that Gernot was thinking: Why is this delightful demimondaine dating a plebeian? Shouldn't she be with me? But I know now that no one on Earth, or at least no one outside the grounds of the Playboy Mansion, is as venal as I am, and that he was entertaining thoughts so radiant and lofty that I couldn't begin to conceive of them: That since the church runs most day care centers, it would have to take the lead in hazel dormouse monitoring. You can't count dormice without an army of very short people to look for empty hazelnuts. My preoccupation with my internal monologue—the sort of thing it is always better to write down than to indulge in at dinner—had blinded me to competing subtexts.

Olaf nodded and voiced his agreement. "Birds are key indicators of intact ecosystems, but small mammals are the staff of life."

"I hope that's large mammal," I said, pointing at the bologna salad.

Olaf began to aver that vegetarianism misses the mark in a country where grazing has helped maintain biodiversity for thousands of years, but before he could tell me anything else I already knew, his phone vibrated.

He excused himself and walked out into the stairwell.

I pulled his plate toward me and arranged several strips of marinated bologna on a slice of gray sourdough. I said, "Olaf knows all about birds."

"He is an expert," the priest said. "But you have not been in Europe for long. You will find that almost anyone can show you many things, even a little child."

"My husband knows all about birds," I said, offended. "I don't need a child to tell me about birds."

"Birds are not indicators," he said. "They are ends in themselves. But now is not a good season for birds. I can show you nuts, berries, and roots. Would you like to come into the forest tomorrow?"

"Tomorrow I'll be busy with Olaf," I said. "Perhaps another time."

"You should come again in the spring," he said. "I would very much like to show the birds and amphibians to someone as sensitive as you are."

He didn't seem the least bit perturbed that I was neither aging nor androgynous. His soft preacher eyes rested on mine as if to say, Do me now, thou tramp.

I should say in my own defense that German girls, even very respectable ones, call the procedure for getting an educated man into bed "*aufreißen*." You rip him open, like a bag of chips. Otherwise he just sits there, giving you to understand through a series of guarded observations that sex is not entirely comme il faut. I.e., every word Gernot said gave him plausible deniability.

I thought, Like all educated Germans, this man treats feminine wiles like fresh chewing gum on the sidewalk and dispenses compliments as if he had been hired as middle management by God, yet unlike the others he is uninterested in forcing me into the kind of serious conversation I am incapable of having. He wants to show me berries!

Or was he kidding, making a joke that would have been understood by someone capable of subtlety?

I didn't know. All I could do was feel his eyes on mine and give it a sexual interpretation. I was to be pitied, although I liked him very much.

"Do you know the Holy Roman Empress Tiffany?" he asked. "She came here from Byzantium to marry Otto the second and was demonized for taking baths and eating with a fork."

I had my unambiguous offer. I glanced away from his eyes momentarily to take in the rest of him.

And there I saw that he was on the old side. Fifty at the absolute minimum. What's more, he knew it, and he was treating me like a kid. Not the mindless whore I naïvely accused myself of being, but a bright and pretty child, one he rather liked. And all at once I recognized him. He had been in Lenzen, at the bar in a clerical collar, discoursing to the drunken masses on how frogs find love.

I awoke from my democratic slumber—my stubborn conviction that everyone regards me as an equal—and ran upstairs to find Olaf. He and his little shoulder bag were gone. I could have gone out earlier to see what he was up to, instead of sitting there mulling over the notion of trading him for a guy old enough to have potency issues. Like any sexual partner, Olaf was unable to compete with the allure of novelty. But that was not, strictly speaking, his fault. I had forgotten his existence almost as a thought experiment. And now he was gone, and I was stuck in the boondocks with a twit who made fun of me to my face. The bus only runs on weekday mornings to take kids to school, and hitchhiking was out of the question, given the traffic density.

I decided to run faster than Olaf could drive. People do it in movies all the time. I skittered back downstairs from the room, took the front stoop in a flying leap, and ran the cobblestones the length of the village, down the middle where they were sort of halfway smooth. And there he was, idling at a bus stop around the corner, talking on the phone. I slowed to a walk. He saw me and waved me away.

I stood next to the driver's side window, raised my fist to knock, and thought better of it. I looked around. A nearby house lowered its blinds. Presumably Breitenhagen had not witnessed a public scene on this order in a while, not since its last unhappy wife raised her voice in mild complaint in 1805. It was that kind of idyllic place.

Olaf finished his conversation. He rolled the car window down and said, "I can't see you right now. I need my space."

"I need you here," I said.

"I need to get home," he said firmly.

He put the car in gear and accelerated, speeding away past a field of geese and what had once been winter wheat. The geese rose in a single chaotic clump, honking and shoving, and flew off across the river as if somebody had slapped them, flying at least half a mile before each one managed to find a slot behind another and form the customary Vs against the pale western sky.

I turned and walked back toward the motel. Then I veered to the left, down the knoll into the frost-dusted fields, my eyes smarting with heat and cold.

I was headed toward the river, I don't know why. But I didn't get very far. In a buckthorn hedge, I saw a family of long-tailed tits. The white-headed, Scandinavian kind. Fluffy, spherical, high on carotene. Like the water snakes, but way cuter as they flowed through the twigs looking for a place to sleep. I stood as though rooted to the ground, or rather as though connected to everything around me by guy-wires in three dimensions. As though

I, they, and the earth were all integral parts of an indispensable scenery.

Space, as any Kantian can tell you, is not forever. A struggling lover can demand his space and then want to see you again in two minutes.

And that's how it was. I snuck past the restaurant to our room and washed my face. Olaf came back, still in his space. The chasm that separated us was no impediment to anything in particular. After all, it had been there the first time we jumped on each other like bugs. The difference was that now we knew about it.

He left again in an hour and said he would tell his wife it had been foggy.

The next day the man of God showed up at breakfast and took me for a walk. The berries were dried on the stems, the nuts were acorns and a few dank walnuts, and the roots were slimy, but it was beautiful.

Only a week later, the Reverend Gernot invited Stephen and me to his paternal home in Dessau to stay overnight. He fed us noodles in the dining room and opened three bottles of wine.

His parents had lived in a thick-walled mansion. The yard had old tulip poplars and dawn redwoods standing in a wilderness of brambles and volunteer pines. A small circle had been mown with a scythe to make room for a bench that faced a mass of feral rhododendrons across a pond with a fountain. There was one rotting birdhouse, nailed to an aged apple tree that had never been pruned. We could see it all through the veranda doors. He talked about the Steckby-Lödderitzer Tree Farm, central Europe's largest remaining contiguous riparian forest. How the river, channeled by inflexible banks of stone, was eating ever deeper into the substrate and taking the groundwater with it, leaving the oaks and alders dead. How sad that would be. He spoke of silvery white willows and plovers. How the riverbanks, left to themselves, would play host to swallow populations adequate to make a dent in the mosquitoes. How ironic it was that Global Rivers Alliance never mentioned the Elbe, simply because it went on for hundreds of miles without a single dam. How easy it would be to take down levees built in the middle ages. You wouldn't need heavy equipment. Just a shovel.

Ça veut dire, civil disobedience. Instead of blather in cyberspace, facts on the ground.

For Stephen, the idea of direct action was like a cross between chocolate cake and the onset of mania. "Frat boys in Patagucci hoisting banners and calling it sabotage," he mocked. "Calling it direct action because it goes directly to the evening news. You know their big idea for the Elbe? A raft. Like they're really gonna make it to the North Sea against the wind. These people embarrass me. But Gernot's tear-down-that-wall thing, that is some serious shit. Respect!"

And thus it came about that armed with free time, relative solitude, and a pickaxe, we quietly set about dismantling the stonework that separated the Steckby-Lödderitzer Tree Farm from the Elbe.

Now, if you compare the stakeholders in the Steckby-Lödderitzer Tree Farm to the twenty billion denizens of cyberspace (that's counting the duplicates), the potential audience for an act of sabotage looks vanishingly small. But Gernot had succeeded in weaving a fuzzy web of universal moral precepts that made even small-time vandalism stretch to the ends of time and space and beyond. I suppose that's what theologians learn in school. For him, we must have been a refreshing change from activists who plan sit-ins in parks where it's legal to sit and schedule vigils for Saturday nights. We didn't pray for peace or play "Imagine" on the autoharp. We were the real deal. Birke could man the tables at the global car wash and bake sale.

He put us up at his dacha in Breitenhagen. It was basically one room, with an entry and a pantry and a niche to sleep in. It was heated, but with a strange stove where you had to dump kerosene on a cookie sheet and drop a match on it. The electric stovetop didn't quite work, but there was a new electric teakettle.

Sabotage was hard labor in damp cold. Under the dirt, the dike was made of rocks the size of pomelos. I cleared detritus and yanked out grass by the roots, and Stephen wielded the pickaxe.

I was good for a two-hour shift. Seeing Stephen heave rocks, I felt I was not of peasant stock. I had narrow little hands like a lemur. Even my opposable thumbs were a work in progress.

After a week, our having hewn a gap in the dike wide enough to flood the neighboring swamp but with no outlet downstream, so that rather than saving the forest we might be replacing valuable wetlands with a lake, Stephen had had enough. He called me over to the bathtub.

He had found, on a shelf, a report by the Macedonian Ecological Society on the avifauna of the FYROM, and had noted glaring omissions in the area of woodland birds. "Look at this list! There are only three hundred and ten species on it. It's like a field guide to the beaches of Macedonia."

"Isn't Macedonia landlocked?"

He continued unerringly. "Reading this, you'd never know the place had trees. There could be anything in there. I've been thinking a lot about my involvement with GRA. I'm not a new-media person and I never will be. That whole holistic, we-are-the-world, network-of-nodes thing. Getting all keyed up about the interconnect-edness. I don't actually get it. My whole training was about last-ditch interventions for people with prognoses so bad you could get regulatory approval for a marlin-spike and crazy glue. I was doing unskilled labor, on a meta level. Meta-unskilled work, like a Rube Goldberg mousetrap with five hundred moving parts. So the whole time with GRA I'm missing the fact that I have skills. There's a kind of biologist I already *am*. Avian population ecologist!" He rolled over to face me, seizing the gunwale of the tub with both hands as he sought eye contact. "So I'm a bird-damaged fuck. So what? Bird damage is a good thing! Plenty of people out there can't tell a willow warbler from a chiffchaff! Liking thousands of birds enough to be able to tell them apart is of indisputable value, whereas social networking is so repetitive I'm going to go fucking crazy, and it's making me nearsighted, which is just what a birder needs. I was getting carpal tunnel syndrome from mousing even before we came to the bayous of Siberia." He held up his right wrist. "My mom told me if you smoke weed you won't get it, but it's not working."

"Your mom told you to smoke weed?"

"No! She told me drummers smoke weed to keep from getting carpal tunnel syndrome."

"I thought they did it because drumming is boring and monotonous."

"It's not monotonous if you smoke weed. What I'm getting at is, wouldn't counting birds down in Macedonia be a lot better use of my time? Who else can listen to birds and say what they are? Not a lot of people. If I stay here on the chain gang, I'll be too crippled to even jerk off."

"I thought you had a girlfriend."

"Nah. Gernot's got her number. He says she's a screech owl."

He had joked that his defection would go unnoticed. There was certainly no sign of life from GRA during his week in Breitenhagen. If the partner organizations missed him reading their press releases, they didn't show it. He returned to Berlin to prepare for his surreptitious self-transfer.

*

Preferring Breitenhagen to Berlin, I proposed a shift in the focus of the project. I explained to Gernot that there was no point in simply flooding the woods, ecologically desirable as that might be, because no one would ever know. I wanted to take the stone cladding off the banks so they would wash out completely. I wanted ships to run aground. I argued that sabotage, being surreptitious, is not nearly as ecclesiastical as civil disobedience, where the point is to get caught.

He raised his eyebrows and said, "I'm not a martyr."

"You don't understand. That's how civil disobedience works. You get punished by the authorities for doing the right thing, and then the papers expose their corruption and stoke the fires of public outrage."

"Having a free press doesn't mean anyone cares," he said. "My central insight of the past twenty years."

"Your congregation will back you up!"

"They'll fire me, and then who will listen to me?"

"I don't know. Me?"

So when the weather wasn't too inexpressibly horrible, maybe twice a week, I snuck out and pried a few rocks off the shores of the Elbe, which soon began to remind me of the pyramid of Cheops.

When I heard a boat, I hid. Every afternoon a little cutter from the WSA (water and shipping office) in Magdeburg steamed by on a tour of inspection. But they must have needed glasses, because they never slowed down.

There wasn't much else in the way of boats, just the occasional half-empty Czech steamer with a skipper staring dead ahead in a trance. Gernot said they paid more attention to riverside goings-on in summer, when I likely would have been naked.

Stephen and I had started on the landward side and piled the fruits of our labors on the ground, anticipating that the eventual cease-and-desist order would include demands for restoration and restitution which might be fulfilled more easily if we could find all the rocks. It was punishing, especially with one of those wheelbarrows with the wheel way out front so you carry half the weight yourself. Alone, I found myself working a little differently. I needed both hands to move a rock, even with a long pry bar. It was easiest to just let them roll into the river.

To my surprise, Gernot looked at the ruined riverbank and was well pleased. Apparently it had never crossed his mind that sabotage doesn't look criminal if you get a young, middle-class housewife to do it. I looked like Jane Birkin in *Slogan*, if *Slogan* had been set in a scout camp in Poland. I worked the way Patty Hearst would have robbed banks if she'd never met the SLA. The militant wing of Global Rivers Alliance radiated innocent industry. If I have one talent in the world, that's probably it. Looking innocent enough to make whatever it is I'm doing appear legal.

Gernot said there was no turning back. "This will be a godsend for the riparian ecosystem," he said. "The river will gently flood the forest and raise the groundwater. No one will ever know. They'll just wonder in a hundred years why the forest is still alive." He occasionally helped me with an especially large rock, but never for more than three minutes before he would see something compelling on the ground or in the air and start rhapsodizing. For him, nothing in nature was distracted or lazy. Every nematode was pulling its own weight, the best way it knew how. It put his attitude toward me into perspective. He praised me with the same effusion he bestowed on chicory, voles, freezing rain, etc.

Every so often he would mention Jesus. Not in a Christian way for American ears; back in the GDR, dissent of any kind had made a person a de facto Christian. It was safer to be at odds with the authorities if you had a consulate to call. The crucifix on his lapel had symbolized access to a mimeograph machine and a telephone that wasn't wiretapped. When its protective spell wore off, around time to do army service, he took up theology per se. He would have liked to know something about biology, he said, but it was not to be. His compromise was to keep a beat-up copy of *Diversity Through Flooding* displayed prominently on his dashboard. He claimed it was impossible to write a sermon without it.

Somehow Olaf could handle my being happily married, but my living in Gernot's summerhouse after Stephen left for Macedonia made him quite insane. He came in the cottage door unannounced, pushed me against the wall, and said, "Why? Why?" He pinned my arms and squished me painfully, almost smothering me, literally, with kisses.

I had to turn my head to get a chance to answer: "Why what?"

"Why are you living with that old goat?"

"Because I'm tearing down the walls of the Elbe as civil disobedience to liberate the Steckby-Lödderitzer Tree Farm?" I said.

It took some explaining. He hadn't known. When I was done explaining, to the best of my ability insofar as I understood the project, he looked more upset than before.

"Good God. It's so dumb. What are you going to do next, spike the trees? This will set the dike relocation effort back ten years. Whose idea was it?"

I, correctly, blamed Gernot.

"This is the wrong time for radicalism on the Elbe," he said. "It's all wrong. It's the Rhine you should be fighting for. Weren't you busy trying to renege on the treaty of Versailles? What happened?"

"That was your old girlfriend," I said. "I say forget the Rhine. It's past saving. It's a drainage ditch. The Elbe is where it all goes down. I like the Elbe. It has real cable ferryboats, not the tourist kind. It has dioxins and nuclear waste. It makes the other rivers seem so plastic."

He hung his head. "Why didn't you tell me? I could have talked some sense into you. The Tree Farm is year-round osprey habitat. Do you know you're disturbing ospreys?"

"Gernot told me to keep quiet."

"The Elbe is Germany's last free-flowing river. Nine hundred cubic meters a second. It's way out of your league."

I frowned.

He was silent, briefly. Then he piped up, "You do know Gernot was an IM, right?"

An ee-em, short for *inoffizieller Mitarbeiter*, meaning unofficial employee: an East German Stasi informant who entrapped friends and neighbors for the sake of professional advancement.

"That's impossible," I countered. "The guy never worked a day in his life."

But it seemed plausible enough. If a guy has a fancy job in the public eye (German preachers are civil servants and Wittenberg is not the most obscure venue), and all he ever talks to you about is the oft-overlooked beauty of voles, etc., you could get suspicious. You could start wondering whether you're apprenticing with an anarcho-sensualist renegade or just easily led.

In Olaf's view, Gernot must be doing something to get off, and it was more likely to involve my ass than voles, while his media-shyness suggested one thing only: guilt. Olaf didn't believe in the innocence of people with critical faculties. The injustice of mortal existence cried out with greed for euphoria. Delicacy had no place in Olaf's world.

It was a difficult discussion. But eventually Olaf weighed his life's work against the value of keeping me off the streets of Berlin, and my lax morals won. The ospreys would have to take a back seat, because he and I were that most common of endangered species: adulterers. The love that dare not speak its name. Not so long ago, it would have been legal for Stephen to shoot us on sight. We had to stick together. As for Gernot's being a Stasi fink, when I brought it up, Gernot got mad. As in really angry. He demanded to know what person of despicable character, compared to whom pig-dogs are models of rectitude, would stoop so low as to retail an accusation that had made the rounds in 1990 but was disproven more conclusively with each passing year, since by this time everybody and his brother had pored over Stasi files looking for evidence of persecution (if it turned out they had targeted you, you had joined the democratic resistance retroactively, which is definitely the easiest way), but none had yet unmasked him.

"Olaf?" I said tentatively.

Gernot looked grim.

"Olaf!" I added, realizing that Olaf could have lied.

On Christmas I talked with Stephen on the phone. He said Macedonia was cold, but not as bad as Kamchatka (meaning Breitenhagen).

On New Year's I went up to Berlin to check up on our apartment. It was fine. Stephen's scholarship kept paying out, and we had set up our bank account to pay the rent and utilities automatically, so it was actually turning a small profit.

I only spent two nights. It was dark and freezing. Neighbors I'd never seen before were setting off bottle rockets in the courtyard.

And thus it was that I acquired red cheeks and pit-pony-like endurance and became inured to physical pain. I spent every thaw heaving rocks into the river from its steep banks, trying not to be dragged in myself by their weight. I hammered on stubborn seams with tears of frustration in my eyes, slowly coming to understand *The Gulag Archipelago* and *The House of the Dead*. I spent entire days commuting between the bed and the bathtub, convalescing.

By mid-February, the gap in the cladding of the banks really was fair size. Most of the rocks were at the bottom of the river, having who knows what effect on it—speeding its flow (bad), slowing its erosion (good), one or the other, depending on whether you listened to Olaf or Gernot.

I experienced the transition from winter to early spring. I saw the moss turn green. Really green, from bottle green to kelly green, with long silky feelers and fur. I heard birds throw themselves into relentless singing the moment they felt the approach of dawn. I saw robins kick rival robins when they were down. Life surged into the trees from below, reddening their twigs. I saw the first bugs on their first forays. All around me, frost was turning to slime. I was looking muscular and outdoorsy and more like a birdwatcher's dream date (the sort of biologist who spends months alone in tern colonies) than ever before. Except for occasional phone calls from Stephen, I hadn't spoken to anyone but Gernot for months, and my German was getting good.

In late March the snow melted in the Czech Republic, and the river rose. Shipping started up again. The bank from which I had removed the granite facing slumped a bit, but no water entered the forest.

I started working on gap number two, though the plan seemed more trivial than ever. The enduring influence of Olaf. He had worked on the dike relocation at The Evil Place, which took years and cost millions, and was an adviser to the Federal Foundation for the Environment, which made NABU and the BUND look like Global Rivers Alliance. And he had parted from me seething, as if I had committed some idiotic stunt like dropping car keys off a boat and would never be a whole person in his eyes again.

Gernot, his hands folded on the table, explained to me that freelance environmentalists had been gravitating toward Germany's northeast corner for twenty years. In the four months between the first free elections and the hostile takeover by the forces of capitalism, East German activists, working feverishly, had established wildlife sanctuaries that were exceptionally large by German standards. But their trusting ways, inexperience with money, confidence that the meek would inherit the earth, etc. left them disqualified to manage their own conquests, rolling out the mat for carpetbaggers like Olaf.

I decided the two men weren't very fond of each other.

I stopped working in mid-April and took up the sweet life. I rode Gernot's bike to all the lakes and checked out every bar in every village.

I missed Berne, but I was not one to hang my harp on the willows and weep. I could easily imagine living in Breitenhagen forever, as long as no one expected me to earn a living. The tap water was delicious, and Gernot kept me in rabbit lettuce, rolled oats, and assorted tubers.

One highlight of the springtime was the annual Elbe Conference in Magdeburg. I got to see Gernot in full effect as a clergyman, which involved eyebrows drawn into a high inverted V. It was a look of deep concern for all mankind, or in this particular case for taxpayers naïve enough to be suckered into shoring up the sagging banks of the forever wild Elbe. The presenters were a mixed bag, from lobbyists and businessmen to a Czech diplomat and the head of the WSA. The Czech attaché cited the Congress of Vienna. The civil engineer said he was just following orders. A BUND activist argued that the Elbe corridor already had perfectly serviceable rail lines, and a soda ash magnate countered that his transportation costs might be marginally lower if the railroad had competition from a canal that would require an initial public investment of only a hundred and fifty million euros. A guy from the railroad wondered aloud what they thought they were talking about, since the soda-ash magnate had his own fleet of trucks and the existing rail line was slated to be scrapped. And so it went on, everyone contradicting everyone else with conflicting incontrovertible facts.

Gernot nursed a look of heartfelt sympathy throughout. His task was to contribute spiritual gravitas. There were pads and pens lying around, so I made note of a couple of things he said. "Energy *sufficiency*, not *efficiency*, is the best means of preserving God's creation." "The Water Framework Directive prescribes explicit process protection for the *morphological dynamism* of God's creation." He said it all in a soft, affectless voice while looking devout, even sheepish. Where was cynical, commanding, slightly loony Gernot? I started to think his job might be tying his hands.

I was hoping to join Stephen in the Balkans, but he didn't want to have me. He said he was free and alone and seeing birds as he had never seen them before. Often seeing every other conceivable thing but birds before realizing what bird belonged where, then applying his new knowledge to identify potentially bird-infested locations and sitting down to wait. Birding at night. Learning new plant communities, new calls, new birds. Talking with friendly Macedonians in no language at all, attending their weddings, riding their ponies.

I objected that it's not safe to ride a pony in sneakers (your feet can slip through the stirrups) and that he's too big for a pony, but he said he had boots and the ponies in Macedonia are called horses. I found the boots troubling, as well as his willingness to believe untruths about animals he was sitting on, but he sounded so happy.

He called me from phone booths. The smartphone with the birdcall apps was gone by day ten, about the time he maxed out his car rental budget, so he recorded his birds on paper. He went native. The way he painted it, he was walking day and night like Robert Walser or De Quincey, crisscrossing the Baba range on scraps of funding mysteriously channeled from Swiss petroleum derivative heirs to Euronatur to a BirdLife partner organization that consisted of a veterinary student named Trajco to him, fit as a fiddle and happy as a grig, leading his feisty pack "horse" up fans of scree until his boots wore out. A confirmed career birder, prospecting for rarities that would be worth their weight in eminent domain once Macedonia joined the E.U., a hero-in-waiting who would shield future UNESCO heritage sites from hydropower with the magic of the Flora-Fauna-Habitats Directive.

Then it was June and he came home to go cold turkey on our couch in Berlin.

Which reminds me of something I maybe ought to point out about Macedonia. It's a major opium producer, which I can imagine being a major attraction for Stephen. He had never mentioned it on the phone, but why would he.

*

I was sorry to leave Breitenhagen. The village sits on a knoll above a narrow bit of floodplain. Huge oaks shade the wetlands. The sun sets when it sets and not a minute sooner. That is, the same sun that slips behind mountains in Berne still white, and behind buildings in Berlin while fading to yellow, there rages orange and pink through the trees and melts to the horizon like a sun going down over the sea. The mist rises off the river, the already silvery willows and poplars go into silver overdrive, the wall of leaves shimmers, and the magenta sun proclaims, LSD Is A Crutch.

In August my sister was supposed to show up in Berlin, but I ended up visiting her in Tukwila. It happened because I went to Albania with Stephen in July. He said that with me to look over his shoulder he'd think twice about even ordering a beer.

There are only two ornithologists in Albania, so prospectors are welcome. You can get a feel for what's out there by checking the market stalls in Shkodër, assuming you can identify birds without hearing their calls or songs, or seeing them stand up, or fly, or with their feathers on.

Organizing the hunters might have helped save habitats. But in Albania only the foreign investors were organized. The Moraca Gorge, for instance, was slated for destruction, with hydroelectric turbines that would theoretically (or rather: impossibly) churn through more water than is in all of Lake Scutari's tributaries combined.

Birke would have been ranting a blue streak. But Stephen just sat there, motionless by the river for days, counting birds on feeding flights. Then he sat by the lake and counted birds in the littoral zone the dam project will eliminate. Fighting entropy the only way he knew how, with tick marks in a notebook.

Now, day trips to the Berner Oberland are one thing, and long weeks of inaction in the piping hot hills of Albania quite another. Nothing against birds, but I had gotten used to moving around a lot. I couldn't do lazy anymore. Even the helpmeet act was getting old. And Stephen didn't need my help carrying stuff if he never moved.

Finally we went down to Ulcinj in Montenegro, where he could do the start of fall migration (honey buzzards) in the salt works and I had English tourists to talk to. And there one of them got me pregnant—a slender, girlish thing of nineteen, funny and whimsical. It dawned on me too late that such things are not always masters of coitus interruptus. I suddenly missed the no-fault abortions of the land of the free. In Germany, it's illegal to discriminate against someone for having the wrong father, so you have to whine about how childbirth would be mental cruelty. Even Albania makes you get counseling. I was hoping for the kind of clinic where you buy a ticket from the cashier and hand it to a nurse's aide without saying a word.

I told Stephen flat out why I wanted to go to Tukwila. He said he didn't care whose baby it was. But I cared, a lot. I flew from Podgorica to SeaTac, which took a while, involved layovers in Bucharest, London, and Atlanta, and was no fun. I got my period on an airplane toilet. I disembarked pale and limp, and that was that.

There are terrible things that never get easier, and there are things even more terrible that get easier with time and repetition. Tukwila is one of the former, a staunch bulwark of defiance against the forces of rationalization that would shred the fabric of the universe to lint. I caught the bus from the airport with a young woman whose hair was lacquered into a ponytail as hard and shiny as a shrimp. Her telephone conversation with her mother revolved around small change that had vanished from her pants pocket the last time her mother did laundry. In addition, her boyfriend owed her eleven dollars, which didn't make her mother's malfeasance any easier to take—au contraire!

You couldn't call it poverty, not of the spirit, anyway. There was nothing slatternly about her. Her look had been designed and executed as precisely as any Caduveo matron's. She chose every word with care, and eventually came to an understanding with her mother, who agreed to lift the disputed amount from the boyfriend's wallet the next time he came around. Her fingernails were glossy claws. Her skin was nearly as shiny as her hair. Her voice had the same stentorian sheen. She may have been twelve. Coming from a subculture in which a pose of stubby-pawed, forthright naïveté is held to embody youthfulness right up to death from old age, I couldn't tell.

My sister had been happily in love with a loaded doctor, but she was way too big a feminist to be a parasite like me. When they broke up because she wasn't making enough money to go skiing in the Andes with him on weekends or help him buy a house on the sound, she ended up in a former motel on Eastlake. But the city had no jobs for classics majors, so she got a job in Tukwila. Eventually she moved there to save gas money.

Her apartment was on the ground floor, next to an access road. It had high, slot-like windows like a spotter's tower, creating the impression (from inside) that she lived in a basement. It was for security, I think; but I could have kicked my way into her apartment, if I'd put on her platform boots. I mean right through the wall. It was paneling over styrofoam over paneling, with studs every three feet. It was no more solid than a yurt. The floor was moist carpet on a concrete slab. In winter she blasted the heat, and in August she blasted the air conditioning. It still took her outfits days to drip-dry.

Doing extra shifts at the strip club totally stressed her out. She was making enough money to think of visiting Berlin on her own, but she had to dance in a much more athletic manner and almost continually, and the guys were closer than they were in the coffeehouse. Right up in her face, as she put it.

Eventually I had to say something, although I am her little sister and not entitled. I said, "You just spent two entire minutes complaining about how your coworkers are bringing down the neighborhood by getting old. Do you have any idea how that sounds?"

"Give me a break, Riot Grrl," she said. "The T&A industry is not about self-determination. It's a market. I'm in direct competition with these old biddies, and we share responsibility for maintaining each other's value. You have to remember that a stripper is a commodity fetish. You can't have sex with me. I exist to be looked at. So the problem is my legs."

"What about them?"

"Look at them." She stuck her leg out at a high angle and waved it around near my head. "Look at my leg. What do you see?"

"It looks fine," I said. "You have pretty legs. Look how little your kneecaps are. They're almost concave."

"You don't get it," she said. "On stage, you need long legs. Pretty works on video, but I don't want to make videos. I want to make tips. But I can't, because I'm short. Unless I make a video. Then I can be a headliner. My boss wants me to make a video."

Being even shorter, I pondered her tragedy abstractly and could think of nothing to say.

"You know how my legs got like this?" she added. "You give up eating when you're nine because you don't want to be fat like your mom. But mom wasn't even fat! My whole growth spurt, you know where I invested it? In my hips. My pelvis is so wide, I could give birth to a calf. At least you had the sense to get married the first time somebody asked you. You can sit on your ass and keep trying to have a baby until kingdom come. I don't even want to know what kind of guy would marry me now. I was stupid to think I could do any job I wanted and it wouldn't rub off. Now I'm starting to acquire the strip-per habitus, and pretty soon I'm going to be forty-five, preemptively shoving my butt in my fiancé's face so he doesn't shine his flashlight at my tits."

"A life laid waste before it began," I said, quoting Stephen's frequent references to the profoundly discouraging climax of the classic Icelandic novel *Independent People* by Halldór Laxness.

"I wouldn't go that far."

"No, seriously. You act like you're trapped in Tukwila, but I bet your boss is surprised every time you show up for work. I bet your landlord wonders what's wrong with you every time he gets a check! Tukwila is a place people walk away from and never look back."

Tukwila, in my opinion, was the trap in the drain. Nobody lives there voluntarily except people who saw nothing but westerns before their grandfathers pawned their TVs. If your basis for comparison is the town Clint Eastwood paints red and renames "Hell," you might like the suburbs of Seattle just fine. For me, even the city was a stretch. Easterners hear "coffee culture" and think of Vienna, not longshoremen idling their pickups at a drive-through. They don't know the uniform polo shirts at Starbucks are the alternative business model for when you want women customers to let their guard down. They hear "beach" and think of sand, not prefab boat-houses selling onion roses and buckets of beer.

*

Stephen claimed on the phone to be sad I hadn't really been pregnant. "It's true!" he said. "A baby from that needle-dick would have been cute!"

I said I would do my best not to get pregnant again until I saw him. Then I told him the really stunning news: Tukwila was swarming with little tiny birds called bushtits that look like long-tailed tits, only cuter, because smaller. Much smaller, and even cuter.

"No way!" Stephen said. "You told me Tukwila is like a trailer park on the moon!"

"I lied! It's the heart of darkness! There are flickers all over the place! They're nesting in the façade of H-Mart!"

"Flickers! Too cool!" Stephen said.

We had to yell because my sister didn't have a landline or even a real computer. She had inferior versions of everything in the world on her phone—entire news stories that read "Italian Assassin Bomb Plot Disaster" or "Lindsey Surgery Denial Scandal About-Face," Voice over IP, little tiny bushtit-sized e-mail messages from men saying things like "Busy tonight? Me, too" and "Can't stop thinking about last March." Her phone service was a joke, but the price was right. She would have been ashamed to use anything else.

We went out for karaoke that night with some of her colleagues from the coffee place. She sang "Because of You" and I blushed. I sang "Waterloo" and thought of Stephen. I got drunk and told them they should unionize, and my sister told me to shut up and sing "How Soon Is Now," to which she cried.

Out in the parking lot, she said, "Watch me," and waited until we were all staring. Then she ran a few steps and did an aerial cartwheel, landing neatly on the soles of her boots.

We stood dumbstruck and dumbfounded.

"Gymnastics is forever," she said. "It's like riding a bike." She did it again.

We all began to laugh. The strength and beauty of what we had seen was so incongruous. My sister, dancing on air. Levitating like a crane. And without a conspecific anywhere this side of Chicago. I had to get her out of there.

In the car, we tallied her marketable skills. It was a short list: Latin, Greek, exotic dancing, coffee drinks. I said it was very promising. "You would get a job in Berlin so fast," I said. "You would have such a good time. You would meet such cute guys."

"I'm there," she said. "I have nothing to lose."

Most of the time, when people say that, they're sort of kidding, but in her case it was literally true. My sister Constance folded her tents in Tukwila and bought a flight the same day as mine.

Stephen was up near Kosovo, counting fervidly. He had learned to identify birds of prey by the hairballs they coughed up and the precise arrangement of their victims' feathers around a stump. He had a book about feathers and another book about seagulls and the many eerie transformations they undergo on their way from being indistinguishable to being basically identical. There was always something going on—some promising-looking habitat to map for its potential. But Albania wasn't Wörgl. He seldom got close to a live bird. Albanians shoot to kill, and they kill to eat, which makes them less repugnant than non-hungry hunters but more lethal. Birds on the move were invisible and nearly silent. They knew better than to draw attention to themselves. They carried on their courtships like hustlers cruising a church picnic, and defended their territories like Beau Geste.

New migrants weren't always up to date. Big flocks would land, or try to, then circle bewildered while one after another was mown down in a flurry of lead. Some liked the look of Albanian wetlands and decided to molt there—the last decision they would make in this lifetime. Birds were executed for the crime of tasting good or the crime of being stringy and gamy. But the hunters and their decoys and semi-automatics couldn't be everywhere at once, so Stephen found plenty to count.

Or count and revise: thirty-five dunlins that landed, seventeen dunlins that took off, six dunlins that made it over the next ridge—an attrition rate that would clearly result in no dunlins at all one stop later, but maybe the hunters are all on this side today. The potential was what mattered. Even in Canton Geneva, there's always the "first disturber," the windsurfer in neoprene who heads out on the first sunny day in February to divest a lake of thirty thousand birds and leave you extrapolating what might have been. Counting bush meat in the market in Shkodër was just another way of acquiring a basis for extrapolation. If a species can't show itself without being shot at, it's comforting to think it's timid. If no nests have been seen for the past ten years, it's nice to know the species requires perfect isolation to breed. Without the tips of icebergs, humankind would already be very lonely.

I didn't fly on the day I had planned. Constance caught a direct flight to Berlin, and I sat in a coffee shop glued to a laptop.

Gernot had sent me a link to a news story that made my spine stiffen: flooding near Dessau-Rosslau. Destruction on a vast scale. Unknown perpetrators had caused the inundation of the Steckby-Lödderitzer Tree Farm, which was strictly protected, for the love of God! If oaks and alders were to drown, the article threatened, the potential damage would be in the zillions.

Gernot told me to take it easy, but legal issues feel different when you're a foreigner. I imagined getting no farther than a cell in Schönefeld airport before being deported to a pit on Rikers Island. I had always thought major flooding came with the spring thaw. "Those are the Alps," he corrected me gently. The Elbe trickles down from bone-dry sandstone. Its flow is more dependent on the central European rainy season, otherwise known as summer vacation—the reason Germans are to be found in such large numbers in July and August on Mediterranean beaches where it's too hot to move or breathe.

"No baby birds drowned, did they?" I asked. Ground-nesting birds had been a particular concern of mine since I discovered their existence.

Gernot said late summer is bird happy hour, when birds fly around in adults-only flocks, and that I should stop beating myself up.

Mainstream environmental groups weighed in to say that while the execution was sloppy, it's the thought that counts, and riparian forests by rights ought to be underwater every so often. Local people began writing letters to the editor, demanding to know why the dikes and cladding couldn't be removed by the long-term unemployed at union wages. Olaf published an editorial pointing out that the would-be radical environmentalists had made fools of themselves by assisting in a reclamation-compensation measure that would soon be fully funded with attendant trickle-down effects—his usual blend of wishful technocracy and wheels-within-wheels irony, leaving at least one reader depressed, yet confused.

Others wondered aloud where the hunters and the WSA had been all that time. Somebody should have noticed something.

I agreed. We had both expected hunters to catch me red-handed. They're under contract to hunt in the Tree Farm, which is mostly the no-humans-allowed core zone of a UNESCO biosphere reserve. Killing deer and wild boar helps protect young trees, rare fungi, ground-nesting birds et al., at least supposedly. But I didn't see a single hunter all winter. Gernot claimed it was because the hunters aren't allowed to feed the animals in core zones, so there aren't any to speak of.

Except he was wrong. He circumscribed his movement to avoid disturbing the wildlife, so he didn't know the core zone was crisscrossed with wild boar highways like a motocross park. I was secretly glad the pigs were afraid of me. I can't begin to imagine what they all ate. Do pigs eat cannabis? There was lots of it growing back in the core zone.

I flew two weeks late, and arrived to find Constance in bed with Stephen, helping him drink a smoothie.

"We didn't do anything," she said. "He's a complete mess!"

It was getting to be a pattern: blissful happiness in the Balkans, precipitous flight home, withdrawal symptoms. But he had no needle tracks or anything to really give me pause.

Constance had no interest in Stephen, she said. She was in love with Berlin. "This is my town," she said. With the help of a few names he had given her, she already had a go-go dancing gig at the Berghain and was a ticket taker at SO36, an alternative discotheque only a hop, skip, and jump from our house.

I asked for a second opinion. Stephen said, "Obviously your sister is Venus in furs with bells on, but it's you I love."

I shook my head and rolled my eyes. "Obviously. She's been perfecting her sexiness on a professional level for five solid years while I've been learning birdcalls! What did you expect? I mean, I've had better men than you, too, but it's not your job to be the fuck of the century! We're married!"

"That's so true!" he said. At least we had that straight.

I offered to bring him breakfast in bed. While he was eating, he said, "Seriously, we should try to have a family and spread all this stability around. Share the love. And what better time to have a baby than when your sister is living with us?"

"Guess again," I said. "If you think she's going to be a huge help with a baby, you've got another think coming. She's going to be a very popular girl and move out within a month."

He sat up leaning on his elbow to steal foam from my cappuccino with the marmalade spoon, and I involuntarily reached over and petted his head.

"I sometimes think about how I used to just work and work and work like a workaholic," Stephen said. "And the rest of my life was balancing my hobbies. Music and birds. Darkness and light. Did you notice how I've sort of slacked off with the music?"

"I thought it was because you found a way to combine birds and drugs."

He lay back and groaned. "Jesus," he said. "You're right. So much for that."

"So now you figured because you're off Special K, I'd be all on fire to have a baby. As a reward for you being scared straight and not falling in love with the contortionist geisha."

"That's not it either. It was more like I had this whole theory about how, through my activism, I was uncovering the dark side of the birds, which is all the things threatening them. Because if you're into wild birds and their lives in the wild, you can't think of the danger they're always facing as a threat. As darkness. You just can't. There's no point. The Lord giveth and the Lord taketh away. Nobody dies except to feed somebody. All of us are somebody's next meal. But with a river some asshole wants to turn into free money, the Lord doesn't have anything to do with it. So that the absolute worst thing in life, which is death," (he lay back on the pillows and spoke slowly to make sure I understood) "is the only bad thing you can actually ever really accept, because you have no choice. It's never an acceptable option, so you just deal with it. You make a virtue of necessity. The way I'm dealing now with my body being a destroyed piece of shit after I treated it like I could just go down to the machine shop and get a rebuilt one after it wore out. I mean, I accept that I'm mortal, but I had to accept it anyway. What am I trying to say?"

"I don't know."

"Right. So these karst fields in the Balkans that they want to turn into hydroelectric projects, it's unacceptable. Maybe you can accept a tsunami, but you can't accept this. You can't."

"What are you trying to say?"

He sat up again. "That you were right to tear down those levees. I'm proud of you." He put his arms around me and hugged me very tight.

At that point I should have realized that he had some kind of sabotage project in mind, cooked up in long hours of staring at empty skies over remote Balkan villages while coked to the gills on whatever, but I was too busy wondering who had washed him in the blood of the lamb.

Working the door at SO36, Constance met a German-American party girl from Minnesota via Bad Homburg who put her in touch with the principal at an English-language private school, and after about a month in Berlin she started working as a fifth grade Latin teacher. The school set her up with a work visa and even wrote her résumé. The kids loved her, the parents loved her. She said she could get me and Stephen a deal on tuition. She rented a sunny fifth-floor walkup in Prenzlauer Berg and started dating a management consultant who practiced Tibetan Buddhism. She was making maybe sixteen thousand dollars a year after taxes, but she wasn't on welfare, so in Berlin she was solidly middle class.

Meanwhile, Stephen and I were reaching new heights of brokeness. George had noticed that Stephen's activities bore only a tenuous relation to Global Rivers Alliance and hired Birke, who was nearly done with school, to replace him. I put in for another grant from the Tiff Foundation (that's what I called my own money from before I got married) to cover my clothing allowance. I wasn't eager to spend money on Stephen.

He suggested I get a job. Or rather, he said, "You know, that school where your sister works is K-12. If your sister can teach fifth grade, you can manage at least kindergarten, can't you?"

"Fie upon you," I said. I had been experimenting with hopeless attempts to muddle through Sir Walter Scott, but mostly getting nowhere.

"Seriously, man," he said, "I need cash to go back to Albania for the international waterbird census. I mean, if Constance can go-go dance, can't you do something slightly less humiliating? Like working the door somewhere? I know so many people who would give you a job."

I put on a turtleneck with little owls on it, a blue cashmere sweater, and green gabardine slacks, clamped my hair into a bun, and went down to interview at SO36. I didn't mention Stephen and said nothing about being Constance's sister. They gave me a job anyway. I had returned to the world of work.

SO36 had a politically correct door policy. Even the drag shows were packed with minority guys who couldn't get past the bouncers anywhere else. So it wasn't long, maybe a month, before I saw a familiar face in the ticket window. It was Elvis, beaming with joy. He bounced up and down, he was so thrilled to see me. He said, "Tiff! Tiff! My love!" I said nothing. He plunked down five euros and I made change. "How are you? I think of you all the days. What you make now in Berlin? What you do later?" He extended his hand into my cage to be stamped.

I held his fingers and rolled the rubber stamp across the tendons of the back of his hand in slow motion, thinking, This is the man I had the best sex with of anyone in my entire life?

When my shift ended, I slunk out like a joker-slash-thief with my collar up and my hat pulled past my eyebrows. I woke Stephen to tell him I had quit my job. I distrusted my body for the first time ever.

Maybe my mind knows best! I thought. This unaccustomed thought shocked me. But I seriously considered it.

And I realized it was true. My body was swept away by the force of the thought like petals blowing off a rose. And there, at the center of the flesh, were the stamen and the pistil, sexual organs seeking not contact but exchange. Not to be pink and velvety-soft and oblivious, but to broadcast and receive spiky, irritating bits of information. The brain, wired to battle entropy with such resolve that anything repeated too often must become imperceptible or be violently rejected. Knowledge, an allergen. Boredom, the mind's spring flood, the sole conceivable force for good, the sole means—for human awareness—of striving toward complexity. Diversity through flooding. Or something, because the allergy metaphor tended to make the spring flood be tears and snot, which couldn't be right. I felt overwhelmed by a new mystic rationalism. I felt a great love for Stephen.

*

Stephen had a plan. Or rather, he had a desired outcome. The result of his efforts would be a Croatian conglomerate's abandonment of a particularly sinister hydroelectric project in the Neretva Delta, and the plan was—was—he didn't know.

"I could have told you that," I said. "You can't sabotage something that only exists on paper."

His eyes lit up. "That's it!" he said. "I have to go after something they've already built."

After several days of reflecting, flat on his back in bed, he had decided on a target: Buško Jezero. He was in transports, overjoyed at his own ingenuity. He was going to build an absolutely huge bomb with manure and diesel fuel and blow up the dam, blocking the canal and disabling the hydroelectric plant so that the waters of Livanjsko Polje would fill the caves like they're supposed to instead of powering techno bars in Dubrovnik.

"It's sort of like what we did at the Steckby-Lödderitzer Tree Farm," I conceded, "except we didn't use a huge bomb. Somehow or other I think the public eye is going to look a little differently at any project involving a huge bomb."

Stephen's eyes glinted in a glassy way. He said, "I guess you're right," and rolled over.

He brought up children again. While slurping a rum and Coke in bed, he said dreamily, "I wish I had fathered a child by accident so now I could find out about it. Like, some cute fourteen-year-old would show up demanding to be told the meaning of life, and she'd be our daughter I didn't know about. You have so many secrets, and my brain is like Swiss cheese, so why not?"

"It could happen," I said. "Perhaps not with me, seeing as how I would have noticed if I had a kid when I was sixteen. It's one of the advantages of being female. But maybe you have like six kids waiting to meet you in Philadelphia and three more in Tidewater, all lining up to collect child support. Maybe that's why you were in such a hurry to leave the country."

"Fat chance. When I met you, I was pure as the driven snow."

"What do you mean?"

"I was a virgin."

"Are you serious?"

"You didn't know?"

"I didn't know. I just thought you were lousy in bed."

"And you married me anyway?"

"You were cute!"

He opened his eyes wide. "Do you have any idea how cute *you* were? I mean, everybody wanted you. You were the unapproachable princess."

"That's crazy."

"Well, whatever else you were, you kept it quiet around the office. Everybody thought I'd won the lottery."

I tried to think back and couldn't. "You can't judge a book by its cover," I said.

"You can if it's never been opened."

"Don't be crass."

"I mean like in *Four Quartets*. The future is a faded song, a royal rose or a lavender spray, of wistful regret for those who are not yet here to regret, pressed between yellow leaves of a book that has never been opened. Like, you as a mom. That's a book that's never been opened. Most things never get opened and just depreciate down to nothing before you even know what they were. Which means life is a total write-down, as in pure profit, everything! Life has an infinite rate of return!"

He looked at me earnestly as if expecting me to know what he was talking about.

I let it pass, feeling I would understand in good time. "So you've had sex with me, Birke, Constance, and Omar's wife. Am I missing anybody?"

"Hey, that's a pretty good track record for a bird-watcher! I know guys with two thousand birds who've never gotten their pencil wet."

"Yecch, Stephen. Where'd you pick up that kind of language?"

"That's standard-issue geek-speak. Not really. But seriously, my grandfather got religion on his deathbed, and he made me swear I wouldn't have premarital sex. And I didn't, almost. Birke would have married me."

"So, like, when you said Constance was the bomb," I said, "you actually had no basis for comparison?"

Not long after, Stephen made another confession. We were perched on a barge on the Spree, enjoying a sunny day with a light fresh wind. We were drinking piña coladas and watching the coots sweep the water with bits of reed held in their bills the way they do, like little brownie scouts sweeping out a parish hall, inept and squeaking, and the DJ had put on Horace Andy ("Skylarking").

"Do you remember way back when," he began, "back in the day, when I saw Birke at Banja Luka with another guy and got all upset? And then I told you she hooked up with your boyfriend."

"Yeah, and Olaf said he never touched her."

"Well, there's a reason."

"Uh, to wit?"

"I was sort of off base about which guy you thought was 'harmless.' You told me you had the hots for a harmless guy. So the whole time in Lenzen" (that is, the half hour he and I were in the same room), "I keep seeing you with a Lutheran minister all into waxing poetic about ecological justice and frogs. You know the guy I mean. And you listening to him all ears and big Bambi eyes and I thought, whoa, Tiff's got a brand new bag! I never thought you meant the fucking *lobbyist!*"

The little gears in my brain were grinding hard. "So after the Rhine Conference," I said, "when you said Birke hooked up with my harmless crush, you meant *Gernot?*"

"I sure as shit didn't mean the swinging dick *lobbyist!*"

I pictured Birke and Gernot together and laughed.

I kept laughing off and on for the rest of the day. I had another fit of giggling while falling asleep. I laughed cruelly at myself, thinking how I had huddled over the cookie-sheet stove in Breitenhagen. I pictured Birke in the rectory in Wittenberg, lounging by the fire on a tiger-skin rug while Gernot brought her hot toddies.

Of course, as Stephen pointed out, they had something in common: rivers. They were both genuinely passionate about rivers. And I'm afraid we performed a number of improvised parodies of riparian hardcore porn over the course of the next several weeks.

I'd like to be able to say we invented riparian porn rather than merely satirizing it, but they say if you can think of it, there's pornography about it, so we can't have been the first. Somewhere out there, there's explicit footage of after-hours goings on at Elbe-Saale-Camp. Which there isn't. I mean, I can't prove it, yet somehow I'm still certain, suggesting to my mind (via Occam's razor) a corollary or rather alternative hypothesis: that all porn is about the same thing, a theme that is unitary, both able and liable to crop up anywhere and be juxtaposed with anything. Stephen had clearly invested a lot of energy in getting Birke to shut up about real existing rivers when they were in bed together—or at least he went to great lengths to include an element of surprise in his oral sex technique, something he had never done before—and found it personally rewarding to construct play-by-play rich in elaborately obscene riparian metaphor, particularly during oral sex when it was especially counterproductive. It all made perfect sense.

*

We went back to Albania in October. Instead of sticking to the coast, we headed up into the mountains by bus—the Bjeshkët e Namuna, the "enchanted" or "cursed" mountains, depending on your perspective.

You can get tired of Albanian buses if you value fresh air or your life. Two villages after Thethi, Stephen suggested horses. I found out something I hadn't known. He couldn't walk uphill. He would take ten steps up a mild grade and then wait.

That sort of explained why he had commuted so cheerfully by car between our first apartment and the corporate campus and didn't like downtown Berne. And why he loved Berlin (flat as a pancake) and never visited my sister. And rented that place that was almost a basement, and drove up roads in Switzerland it had been totally illegal to drive up, and gave the appearance of being addicted to pills: Stephen had a bad heart.

I didn't advertise how dull I was by sharing my belated insight. I just asked what was wrong with the southern coastal wetlands, like maybe Butrinti. He said Italian tourists hunt in packs and he would rather get into shouting matches with one gun-toting maniac at a time.

I favored renting a car. Neither of us knew how to ride a motorcycle. We couldn't imagine making it up the grades with mopeds, but we could easily imagine tumbling to our deaths. Stephen thought a horse would be nice, like he had in Macedonia. Birds like them, and you can fuel up on whatever happens to be growing on the ground. But the scheme turned out to be impracticable. Trekkers had made the "horse" scene a seller's market.

We compromised on a donkey. No ecotourist was heartless enough to ride a donkey, so the price was still relatively Albanian.

I didn't know much about donkeys. My boarding school had a "coon-jumping mule," a term on whose origins I refuse to speculate, and I had ridden it plenty of times when we were giving the thoroughbreds a rest for whatever reason. It could jump over a four-foot fence from a standstill, like a jack-in-the-box. It had nothing in common with this diminutive stoic. With or without Stephen on its back, its pose was the same. Its general demeanor suggested that the burden of Stephen was no heavier than the burden of existence. On steep paths Stephen would dismount and hold fast to its mane, like a climber being short-roped by a Sherpa. It seemed strong as Godzilla. I named it Brighty.

Once I got used to the visuals, there seemed nothing odd to me about a rider whose sneakers almost dragged the ground. Stephen didn't use a saddle, just a folded blanket to keep donkey hair from working its way through his pants. I held the rope and carried our stuff in a back-pack, and we fit right in. Albania is the West Virginia of Europe. Single mothers there dress and live as men.

I identified with Brighty. Her humble patience, her long-lashed eyes, the graceful way she picked out a route to nowhere with her tiny feet. We were one. Stephen told me where to go, and I led Brighty, on whom Stephen sat. A trinity. Three beings with a single will. I had never envisioned myself wearing a backpack larger than my torso and leading my husband through ancient live oaks on a donkey, wowing each village in turn like Christ's entry into Jerusalem, but then again, I never did have much imagination.

Stephen came clean about his Macedonian pony adventure. When he had decided to try riding, the one person in town who knew English and could answer his questions was a Catholic missionary, who referred him to a farmer who had a spare pony. It was spare for the reason that it hadn't been ridden in years. Its shaggy pelt was caked with mud and its hooves needed trimming. Stephen cleaned and filed its hooves, brushed its coat to a fine gloss, and dressed its wounds. He decided it cleaned up pretty good, so he climbed aboard and rode across the fields into a swamp, where the pony panicked, never having been that close to trees in its life. It lay down and cowered, then rolled. He succeeded in calming it, but not himself, as hundreds of deerflies descended and began biting them both cruelly. He improvised blinders and a fly whisk from the surrounding vegetation and remounted. They moved forward. The woods were hot and damp, and they both sweated unconscionably. The pony was unhappy and so was Stephen, so that when it took to sprinting, determined to get out of the trees at any price, he gave it its head. He threw himself to the ground to avoid being killed by a low branch, but he held on to the reins, and the pony didn't drag him more than maybe ten feet. Being Stephen, he then assumed that their relationship had nowhere to go but up.

Since there wasn't much for Brighty to eat, we had to book her into overnight lodgings the same as ourselves.

The farmers sometimes fed her armfuls of leaves ripped off the trees with pruning hooks. Their livestock was goats and sheep with long dreads and ferocious coin-slot eyes. Their cars were egg-shaped from running into rocks.

Albania was no wilderness; there were even marked trails. But it wasn't exactly crowded. We were pretty much left to ourselves. On the way up Pllaja e Pusit, two American-looking guys whizzed past us on mountain bikes doing forty miles an hour without saying a word. They terrified Brighty and made us take an hourlong break during which we saw *Fringilla coelebs* and *Motacilla alba*, two birds you might consider noteworthy if they were to appear in flocks of one million plus or open their mouths and speak. The friendlier tourists were not much better. Without a language in common, no upscale traveler could adequately convey the native wit and creativity that had inspired him to take some travel guide's hint to go to Albania before capitalism turned it into Montenegro. Finns or Tuscans or whatever would remark of Brighty, "Good car!" and we would say, "Good car for good roads!" Everyone would laugh, and they would pet her nose, causing her to stand still for upwards of fifteen minutes so we had plenty of time to discuss the location of the closest good town or good restaurant with good food while uninteresting birds flowed past in waves. We met a group of women from England, but they didn't get the donkey-backpack-surrendered wife thing. We didn't see any more English guys. They were scarce away from the waterfront bars.

Stephen catalogued bird after bird. The only ones you could see clearly were the big BOPs circling out of the range of gunfire. One toted a partridge—Stephen's first and last partridge, it turned out. Most flitted past us like sparks arcing, emitting squeaks that identified them to Stephen but not to me. One day we got to a dead ewe in time to catch the goose-stepping of the griffon vultures arriving to deliver its breech birth along with everything else except its rumen, bones, and pelt. Before I closed my eyes, it skyrocketed to first place on the list of the most repellent spectacles I had ever witnessed, lending a vivid symbolic figuration to events I had hitherto refused to name.

Stephen whispered that he was scanning the periphery for the white Egyptian vultures that specialize in crime scene cleanup, but the steppes were No Bird's Land. Birds were willing to fly in from distant mountain peaks for a free meal, but they didn't care to set up shop. Only the migrants didn't know any better, to their sorrow.

We saw the moa a few times. Stephen would hear it shift its weight in the underbrush, mostly when we were having sex. He would put his hand on my mouth and whisper, "Listen. The moa." He would prop himself up on his elbow and look around. The moa would stand up in the bush where it had been hiding and walk away, reviewing its cell phone video, assault rifle hanging low like a bass guitar.

*

When we couldn't take the mountains anymore, we gave Brighty to a single mother who promised to feed her, and caught the bus headed for Pustec. Just inches from the lumpy rock, there's a smooth, modern road. We flew down—that's how it felt after all that time without wheels, like gliding—and alighted on Lake Prespa in the evening.

We got off at a lonely bus stop in front of an empty hotel. Walking felt cumbersome, like when you take off your skates after hours at an ice rink. We crossed the wide, flat plain of scrub where the lake had once been until we reached the shoreline. The transparent water was so smooth it seemed like a blob of mercury resting in a spoon. The orange sun dyed our shadows on the water blue.

It was clear and cold. Stephen got in as far as his thighs and stood there being a wimp. He started walking forward again and lost his balance. He splashed around for a bit on his knees. He asked, "Is this necessary?" in a tone of irritation and was suddenly underwater.

I thought of sinkholes and underground rivers. He tried to pull himself back to his feet by using the surface of the water as a banister. He went under again. I reached him and pulled his shoulders up. He looked at me, demanding answers. I dragged him back to the flats and nestled his head in gravel. I ran toward the road and back again. I did CPR, which I had learned on a rubber dummy in school, but it was pretty much a joke, since he was mostly in the water, with water in his lungs. And at some point after that he was dead. Of a heart attack, I think, but nobody really knows.

A hunter helped me carry Stephen onto the grass. He called an ambulance while I put on my clothes.

I'm calling him a hunter because he had a rifle, but actually he was just a guy out riding around on a moped. It's not like you'd call every Yemeni with an AK-47 a paramilitary. I mean, obviously he would have shot us if we hadn't been human. That's why you could go for months without seeing any animal other than a bird. Birds are braver than the other animals, because they have an ace up their sleeve: flight. Maybe Europe had flightless birds once, but nobody ever saw them because they hid instead of fleeing. And then they were gone, like the lavender in the book that was never opened. The marbled teal is almost gone. It doesn't hide. It flies away, low and slow and in a straight line.

All in all, I have nothing non-symbolic to say about Stephen's death and will stop now, almost. I had known that dying turns people into an incoherent jumble of meaningless forces that gets rolled round in earth's diurnal course like rocks and stones and trees, because I read it in *The Education of Henry Adams*. Henry's sister dies of tetanus after an accident, and he makes it abundantly clear that nothing could have been more pointless. I hadn't known about ghosts and zombies. I thought they were pop-culture pseudo-folklore that turns up in B-movies because all you need is makeup.

But Stephen kept breathing long after he was dead. Even his feet breathed. And after he was gone, he became a ghost. I would realize he was dead, and feel I'd seen a ghost.

Maybe if Henry Adams had written more about his wife.

Some nice nurse found Trajco's number in Stephen's wallet. Trajco, the amateur ornithologist with a thing for beaches. He arrived a day later. I was sitting in the hospital lobby staring at nothing. Thinking it might help me commune with Stephen, who had become nothing.

Trajco hustled me to a hotel. He more or less sat on me for a day and a night. He assured everyone I would be fine once I was back with my sister in Berlin.

Constance flew out to pick me up in Skopje. Her presence calmed me instantly. She had seen me in worse crises, like spankings for lying to protect her. She had that steadying family influence. So soothing, yet always unpleasant in one way or another. In her case the problem was intimacy and easy familiarity. She confessed that she felt seriously guilty for sleeping with Stephen. I said, Please don't! He really enjoyed it! At which point she got all sanctimonious because whatever else her flaws, she wasn't a swinger, plus she had been really attracted to him, unlike me. At the time it blew my mind that anybody could feel guilty about anything unless he had personally murdered Stephen. But she wanted to feel something; and regarding his existence as over, she went mining for feelings in their shared past and came up with not being sorry she'd fucked his brains out.

By the time we got to Berlin, I decided I'd had enough steadying and wanted to go home. But when I tried to turn the key in the door to our apartment, it kept slipping out from between my thumb and forefinger. I literally couldn't get inside. I went back to Prenzlauer Berg and waited for Constance in a café.

She promised to deal with all the paperwork and so on related to the proper disposal of Stephen's body. And she did. It took weeks. She became my hero.

Omar called. He said, after swearing me to secrecy, that the pump was an artificial heart and Stephen wanted to work on it and that's why he was so desperate to get a transfer to Berlin.

At the funeral, I finally met Stephen's mother. She looked at me with a hatred I'd only ever seen before on a caracal in the zoo.

Stephen turned out to have a major life insurance policy he had let lapse. If I had liquidated the Tiff Foundation to pay our bills in Berlin, I would have been a millionaire.

Gernot invited me to stay in Breitenhagen. Inside: peace and stillness, the cookie-sheet stove, his books. Outside the fields stretched to the horizon and laggard cranes plowed their heavy, slump-shouldered course through the sky, tootling as they went. The moon glazed the Elbe silver and I walked through the snow. Crunch, crunch. Physically, Breitenhagen was the anti-Berne. A world without end. To see a definite horizon, you had to go inside and pull the curtains.

On Boxing Day, while Gernot was at church, Olaf came to see me. He brought flowers and a store-bought cake and set them on the table. He looked older, just like me.

"I doubt you're happy to see me," he said. "I doubt you're happy about anything."

"That's not true," I said. "If I keep moving around, I'm fine, and if I wake up at night, I go out. Then I feel better."

He suggested we take a walk.

I suggested we go to bed, occasioning a stricken look. I apologized.

"Really, it's my fault," he said. "I should have left you alone to think things through."

"No," I said. "Seeing you is a nice surprise."

"Are you really okay here by yourself?" he asked.

I said, "It's weird being alone. I thought I would be married to Stephen forever. It never crossed my mind that we'd ever split up. Not really. It's like I was a part of him, and he was a part of me. We did that classic couples thing, where you delegate functions to each other and end up losing basic competencies, but we were always together, so it was no problem. Now I have to figure out what aspects of myself I let him adopt and represent, and what parts of me are actually him."

"Hmm," he said. "That sounds like a load of pop-psychological bullshit."

"You have a wife," I said. "You know what it's like."

"Had a wife."

I acquired a stricken look of my own. The Olaf of my dreams was a married man and lived on the Rhine. This was the Elbe, and the day after Christmas. I looked down at the flowers. Pink roses. He clearly had something in mind.

He looked at them, too, and remarked, "That was probably the first time in your life a man turned you down for sex."

"Not true," I said. "Some guys can't get it up after two drinks."

While he was demonstrating his sobriety with a rhetorically impressive account of various inner struggles surrounding his divorce, it crossed my mind that, Stephen's being an incubus aside, and beyond his haunting my waking nightmares as a hairy mass of suet in a universe that resounded with screaming, he had abandoned me for Birke and found quite extraordinarily high praise for my sister, while I had respected his privacy so much that I let him outsource his health to a donkey and die slower than Anne Brontë in Mrs. Gaskell's life of Charlotte—i.e., like a dog. When it came to relationships, I concluded, I could possibly take tips even from Olaf. I admitted that what I had just said about being part of Stephen had been a pack of lies.

"That's good," Olaf said. "Because if I catch you being a part of me, I'll give you somebody to be a part of."

It was a proposal of marriage and children. I smiled. My future spread before me like a picnic. I would marry Olaf and study to be an expert on woodlands. He would smile on me beneficently as I grew into the role of well-informed conversational partner and competent working mom. I was liberated from all doubts of my self-worth and said not a word.

We had sex and went for a walk. I leaned my head on his scratchy tweed coat. A woodpecker bobbed up in front of us like an apparition, then tucked in its wings and fell away into the core zone.

Olaf said, "By the way, I live near Berlin now."

I said, "That's nice. I was always wondering when you'd figure out Bonn isn't the capital anymore."

"I work for Global Rivers Alliance."

I couldn't jump away. I pushed hard, but he kept his arm around my shoulder.

"They got a huge grant," he continued. "They have some important donors, defectors from the WWF. It's going to be a powerful organization. Birke's a competent fundraiser, but she needed somebody with liaison experience to do the actual work. You can't just raise money for its own sake."

"No, I guess you can't!"

"Are you upset?"

"Can we go home now?"

"Sure." He turned us around.

"Are you sleeping with Birke the way everybody else is?" I asked.

He sighed. "No. You have a one-track mind. You think Birke needs my help? She's doing me a favor, not the other way around. Life is not fair. Listen, I came here to ask you to move in with me."

"I don't think I can move to Berlin. For one, seeing that stupid twat get rich off Global Rivers Alliance would kill me."

"The GRA office is in Berlin, and my place is in Lehnin."

"Lenin?"

"Kloster Lehnin. It's south of Potsdam. I have bull-finches and wrens. I have squirrels. Come on, say yes. I always wanted a girlfriend with a one-track mind."

I stopped walking and stomped both feet in frustra-tion. I actually hopped in place on the snow like an angry robin. I said, "I am through being people's sex slave! I want to study organic forestry!"

He backed away from me and said, "You really mean it."

"Birke majored in design. She wouldn't know a river if it bit her on the butt. I don't want to be that kind of activ-ist. I want to be the kind that makes a difference! The kind with a policy job! I want an education! I was raised on art and literature, the opiates of the intellectually underprivileged" (here I used the term for the poor in spirit from the Sermon on the Mount), "but I refuse to go on fiddling while Rome burns!"

"The forest service is more hierarchical than the Vatican. They have two missions, to harvest trees and shoot deer. You wouldn't last a week."

"Germany has freedom of conscience! I'll take it to the European Court of Human Rights if I have to!"

"What if I said I adore you? That I miss your fierce volubility every day?"

"What's 'volubility'?" (The German was over my head.)

"My life would be so much more fun if you lived in Lehnin. You can study something sensible in Potsdam. There are lakes everywhere up there. There's a kayak in my shed. I have a big yard. Move in with me, you dingbat. It's half an hour to Berlin. Nothing would remind you of Stephen. You wouldn't even have to see your sister. Global Rivers Alliance is paying me serious money, at least for the first year."

I said, "Okay."

Gernot came to visit. He said he saw it coming. He said, "Olaf knows what he wants. That's normal for a bird, but exceptional in a human being."

"Olaf just wants to breed and feed like everybody else," I said.

"You're underestimating birds," he said. "When he came to see you, did he eat or impregnate anything? False alarm. He came to sing his song."

"Um, you could be right," I said.

"When I tell my congregation there's more to life than food and sex, I'm just singing my song. From over their heads, like a bird in the pulpit, and people respond. No information changes hands, but it doesn't matter.

Preaching really is like birdsong. If you find the melody, the fiction soars upward and joins the invisible truth. People respond to the truth in the lie. The way a bird responds when it hears its song. The males back off, and the females crouch down."

I frowned and said, "The females crouch down?"

He continued, "Tiffany, you must try to understand that it takes conditions of artificial scarcity to make satisfying basic needs seem beautiful. Our society works hard to make food and sex as scarce as beauty and love."

"You're up to your neck in food and sex!"

"So what?" he said. "They can't stop me from being afraid you're leaving."

"I'm not leaving! I'm going to Potsdam. It's like half an hour."

"Of course. And what about when GRA assigns Olaf to open an office in Brussels? I wouldn't be surprised. Do you speak French?"

"Brussels!" I said. "I always wanted to live there!"

"My love, you have the attention span of a fish."

"But I'm going to improve it in school in Brussels. I bet they have international programs in English. In ten years I'll be really educated and purposeful. I don't mean with a one-track mind, like I have now, but a force to be reckoned with, like Olaf or Batman."

He shook his head and let go of my hands. "A butterfly among the birds," he said.

I sat up straight. "Do you mean I remind you of the wallcreeper?"

"No. I meant Olaf is going to feed you to his young."

He picked out two walnuts from the bowl on the table and broke one against the other using both hands. He ate the weaker walnut, then tested the strength of the remaining walnut against a new walnut. It was something I'd seen him do dozens of times. At first I thought he was doing it to kill time in the silence, but after the same walnut won eight rounds I sort of got the picture.

"The strong walnut is boring," I said. "It might as well be a rock."

"It flatters itself that the nutcracker finds it especially attractive," he said, reaching for the nutcracker.

"You're unhappy because I'm marrying Olaf," I said pointedly.

"I'm bitter," he said. "All growing things are bitter." He picked a thin lobe of grayish meat from the ruins of the especially hard nut, turning it this way and that, and set it down again. "Summertime is sour. What is mature turns sweet and falls, like your Stephen. You're in love with endings now. And you believe that for Olaf, you're the end."

"I don't expect him to love me forever. Just long enough to raise a couple of kids."

"Aha. You admit openly that he loves you the most right now. Because you will never be younger, more playful, or more obedient. With luck, your children will supplant you and he will go on loving you for their sake. This is love as a deflationary spiral. A never-ending buyer's market."

"You really are bitter," I said.

*

I went back to Berlin and gave notice to the landlord. I went through Stephen's stuff. I took everything we owned (meaning almost everything but my clothes) down to the flea market by the Landwehr canal and priced it to sell. When evening came, I walked off and left it. I embarked on my new life.

There's a bird called a nutcracker, but it lives on pine nuts. When a bird wants to crack an actual nut, he drops it a long way on concrete.

I.e., Olaf lost interest in sex the minute I moved in. He said it was me, and that being around a grieving widow was bringing him down. When I tried to strong-arm him into taking the Brussels job, he called me a harpy.

I felt I'd never liked him and never known him. And all because he never bent over backward to please me, even though we were together. I had thought that's what boyfriends did. He started spending weeknights in town with Birke. Once she called me up, sounding excited, wanting to have a serious talk between old friends. It was mortifying. I realized they were both complete assholes, and if not for the one, I would never have met the other.

Then he moved out and left me alone in Lehnin. The yard was mostly sheds filled with junk. The neighbors stared at me. The kayak had a big crack in the hull, exacerbated by incompetent repairs.

*

For months I lay like a windfall peach contemplating its own bitter almond.

Then I got up and called Gernot. He sounded delighted. For reasons that resist examination, I began by proposing marriage.

"I will never, ever marry anyone, least of all you," he said. "But you can live in Dessau rent-free if you redecorate. I'll pay for the materials. Isn't that what women want?"

"I could kiss you!" I said.

"Women are all the same," he said. "Inscrutable guardians of inexpressible passions, and sentimental about money."

"I didn't ask you to pay my rent," I pointed out. "I just need you to save me."

"A universal error of women," he said. "True subproletarians, always giving themselves body and soul because they have nothing else. In gratitude for crumbs of power and security that fall from others' tables, helping those who need it least. Helping strong, successful, sexy men, for the love of God." He sighed.

"Isn't letting me live in the house *you* helping *me*?"

"Thanks for the compliment, darling, but you are mistaken. Where that house is concerned, I am the poorest of the poor. No private citizen can afford German craftsmen, and if I hire migrant laborers tax-free like a normal person, I lose my pension. To frame tax evasion as civil disobedience is difficult. Until retirement, I am tied to Wittenberg with chains of steel. The house must be lived in. But I can't rent it out. It's too big. It would need to be to cut up into apartments, and that would break my heart. To sell it would likewise break my heart."

"Can I take up the carpeting?"

He sighed again. "Here is my final offer, Tiffany. Stop following orders. Do what you want. Work selfishly. Without the experience of control, you will never have the experience of creativity. Stop giving yourself away, and you will have more to offer than your body and soul. Keep them and cultivate them. Learn, learn, and once again learn!" He said that last bit in Russian, quoting Lenin: *Uchit se, uchit se, uchit se.* I said I would take it under advisement.

After a while, I decided he might be on to something. I had been treating myself as resources to be mined. Now I know I am the soil where I grow. In between wallpapering, I wrote *The Wallcreeper.* Then I started on the floors. Then I took up playing the piano. I went back to school in Jena and graduated in hydrogeology. I worked for a while at the Federal Environmental Office (it was moved from Berlin to Dessau in 2005, presumably to decrease its influence), and quit to found an ecological planning bureau. I am proud to say that my environmental impact statements have helped make dredging the Elbe prohibitively expensive. It is now silting up and winds lazily among shifting sandbars, very good for canoeing. Children wade out to the islands. The house just keeps getting nicer and nicer. I pack it with furniture to keep Gernot from bouncing around. The movie version ends with a montage of Stephen in bed with different club kids (almost all girls) in Berne. Soundtrack: "Oh Very Young."